"I hope you got what you came here for,"
Laura said sharply.

She regretted the words the moment they left her mouth, particularly when James Paden halted on his way out the door and slowly turned around. He no longer looked like a successful businessman interested in buying a house. He was eighteeen again, wild and undisciplined and dangerous.

He closed the door he had just opened and said, "Not quite."

With one lithe movement he grasped her arms, turned her around, and pressed her against the door. Splaying his hands wide on either side of her head, he leaned forward, his mouth swooping down on hers.

She tried to dodge it, moving her head from side to side. "No, James. No!"

But he was relentless and persistent, and though he wasn't even using his hands, the moment his mouth captured hers in a fiercely hot, open-mouthed kiss, she was defeated. It was one of those ravenous kisses she'd thought only existed in the movies.

When she finally broke free and pulled away from him, she spoke breathlessly. "Why did you do that?"

He smiled with a kind of brazen amusement. "I just thought you needed a good kissing. . . ."

WHAT ARE *LOVESWEPT* ROMANCES?

They are stories of true romance and touching emotion. We believe those two very important ingredients are constants in our highly sensual and very believable stories in the *LOVESWEPT* line. Our goal is to give you, the reader, stories of consistently high quality that may sometimes make you laugh, sometimes make you cry, but are always fresh and creative and contain many delightful surprises within their pages.

Most romance fans read an enormous number of books. Those they truly love, they keep. Others may be traded with friends and soon forgotten. We hope that each *LOVESWEPT* romance will be a treasure—a "keeper." We will always try to publish

LOVE STORIES YOU'LL NEVER FORGET
BY AUTHORS YOU'LL ALWAYS REMEMBER

The Editors

LOVESWEPT® · 154

Sandra Brown
22 Indigo Place

BANTAM BOOKS
TORONTO · NEW YORK · LONDON · SYDNEY · AUCKLAND

22 INDIGO PLACE

A Bantam Book / August 1986

ISBN 0-553-21777-1

Published simultaneously in the United States and Canada

---

*Bantam Books are published by Bantam Books, Inc. Its trade-
mark, consisting of the words "Bantam Books" and the por-
trayal of a rooster, is Registered in U.S. Patent and Trademark
Office and in other countries. Marca Registrada. Bantam
Books, Inc., 666 Fifth Avenue, New York, New York 10103.*

PRINTED IN THE UNITED STATES OF AMERICA

O   0 9 8 7 6 5 4 3 2 1

One

The motorcycle shot out from behind the live oak, where it had been hidden by the wisteria vine. Laura Nolan, surrounded by the dense darkness on the shadowed porch, spun around at the roaring sound of the engine. Flattening herself against the front door in fright, she pressed her fist, which was clutching her front-door key, against her chest.

"Are you Mrs. Hightower, the realtor?" the biker asked.

"No, I'm not the realtor. I'm the owner of the house." A bit more imperiously, she added, "And I don't thank you, sir, for scaring the living daylights out of me. Why were you hiding behind the tree?"

He switched off the key in the ignition. The motor purred to a stop. He swung his leg over the seat of the disreputable-looking machine and sauntered around the rear wheel. "I wasn't hiding. I was waiting. And I didn't mean to scare you."

That was what he *said*. But the slow, deliberate

way he came stalking up the front-porch steps made Laura wonder if he meant it.

She was alone. The place was deserted. She was frightened.

Anybody could have seen the real estate sign posted on the main road and driven up the lane to the house on the pretext of being an interested buyer. How many people went house-hunting on a motorcycle? Mustering the most intimidating tone she could, she said, "If you're waiting for Mrs. Hightower, I think—"

"Good Lord o' mercy, if it isn't Miss Laura Nolan herself."

For several moments she was unable to speak. "How—how do you know me?"

His chuckle—low, throaty, not quite sinister, but dangerous just the same—sent shivers down her spine. He had reached the porch and now stood on a level with her. Except that he was much taller. Much. He seemed to loom over her there in the shadowy darkness. "Now, don't be modest, Miss Laura. Everybody knows the prettiest little rich girl in Gregory, Georgia."

She took exception to several things. His tone of voice, for one. It was offensive, anything but respectful. The drawling inflection was insolent and subtly mocking. Then she was offended by his reference to her family's affluence. Mentioning such things was in the poorest taste, and indicated that he had no manners and little, if any, regard for convention. And last, but most disturbing of all, was the way he moved in on her, backing her up, until her bones were trying to impress themselves into the wood grain of the front door.

The man stood so close that Laura could feel his body heat and smell his cologne. Few people had the gumption to block her path, much less invade her space. She didn't like his impertinence one bit. This stranger was breaking all the rules of polite society. Just who did he think he was?

"You have me at a disadvantage," she said coolly, "because I don't know you." She intimated that she wanted to keep it that way, too. "If you're interested in seeing the house, please wait for Mrs. Hightower here on the porch." She nodded toward the wicker settee. "She's very good about keeping appointments, so I'm sure she'll be along shortly. Now, if you'll excuse me." Laura rudely turned her back on him to unlock the front door.

That probably wasn't the smartest course of action, but she was more perturbed now than frightened. If he had had something criminal in mind, he would have proceeded with it by now. So, at the moment, it only seemed imperative to put space between the man and herself.

She fitted the key into the lock, thanking heaven that it slipped into the hole without her having to stab at it several times because of the darkness. She unlocked the latch and pushed the door open. As soon as she stepped inside, she automatically reached for the light switch and flipped on the front-porch lights. There were three of them, nicely spaced and hanging on long brass chains from the balcony overhead. They flooded the porch with light. When Laura turned to close the front door, she gasped in surprise, partly because the man had followed her as far as the threshold, but mainly because she now recognized him.

"James Paden," she said in a hoarse whisper.

His grin was slow in coming. When it finally did tilt up the corners of that sullen, sensual mouth, it made him look aggravatingly smug. He hooked his thumbs through the belt loops of his jeans, propped one shoulder against the doorjamb and said, "You remember me."

Remember him? Of course she remembered him. One didn't forget characters like James Paden. Such misfits always distinguished themselves in one's memory, if for no other reason than because of their dissimilarity to anyone else.

And unlike anyone else in Laura's memory, James Paden held the distinction of being the only person she knew who had practically been railroaded out of town.

"What are you doing here?"

"Invite me in and I'll tell you. Or am I still denied entrance into the hallowed halls of Twenty-two Indigo Place?"

She took umbrage at his implication that she was a snob and that not everybody was welcomed into her home. Although it was true. Randolph and Missy Nolan would have had conniption fits if their only daughter had invited the likes of James Paden to any of her many parties. "Of course you may come in," she said stiffly.

He pushed himself away from the doorjamb and swaggered past her. "Thanks."

His sarcasm made her grind her teeth, but she closed the door and stood aside while he leisurely and thoroughly inspected the entrance hall of her house. While he was doing that, Laura inspected him.

James Paden. Wild, rebellious, disreputable. He had been the scourge of the public-school system in Gregory until he had graduated, several classes ahead of Laura. The local police department was well acquainted with him too. Oh, he hadn't been an outlaw. Exactly. Just incorrigible.

He and the pack of boys who had followed him around on their motorcycles like faithful knights to an exiled king had claimed the pool hall as their headquarters. When they weren't there, they were on the prowl. They spelled trouble, and everyone avoided them if at all possible. They were known for hard drinking, loud cussing, fast driving, and wild living, this small town's version of Hell's Angels.

The unqualified leader, James Paden, had grown up without discipline, without apparent ambition, without an iota of regard for anybody or anything. Nice young men were advised to stay away from him at the risk of getting into trouble. Nice girls were advised the same thing, only the risks they were taking by associating with him had much more dire consequences. Good reputations and sharing company with James Paden were irreconcilable.

Ironically, he had a magnetic personality. Men and women alike were drawn to him the way they were to any vice. He was exciting and fun. Sinful. Therefore wickedly attractive. All it took was a certain look, a suggestive arch of his brow, one crook of his finger, and susceptible victims, people with no self-restraint and little willpower, flocked to him.

He certainly had had the good looks to go with the alluring personality. Long before they became acceptable, much less fashionable, he had worn tight jeans and T-shirts, a leather jacket with the collar flipped up, and boots.

His saddle-brown hair had always been worn long, and he cared little for styling. He viewed the world through broody green eyes lavishly screened by dark lashes. His mouth was frankly sensual, the lower lip being fuller than the upper. His mouth could be downright pouty when a derisive smile wasn't tugging up one corner of it . . . as now, when he turned and found Laura studying him so intently.

She gave him a vapid smile and said, "Would you like to wait for Mrs. Hightower in the parlor?"

Picking up on her formality, he said, "After you, Miss Laura."

Laura would have liked to wipe that cynical grin right off his face. Her palm fairly itched to make contact with his cheek. Instead she turned her back and led him into the front parlor. She switched on lamps as she went.

He whistled long and low when he entered the room. Standing in its center, he slid his hands, palms out, into the seat pockets of his jeans and did a slow three-hundred-and-sixty-degree pivot on the heels of his boots.

Laura couldn't help but notice that the quality of his clothes had changed, if not the style. The boots, for instance, were expensive. They were scuffed and dusty, but she knew quality when she saw it.

What she didn't want to notice, but what couldn't be ignored, was how little his physique had changed since she had last seen him, over ten years ago. He had filled out, reached his full maturity, but he hadn't gone to fat. He was still slender and tough. His waist was trim, his belly flat, his hips narrow, his shoulders broad, his chest wide. And he still moved with sinuous, predatory stealth. He never seemed to hurry.

"This is some room."

"Thank you."

"I always wanted to see the inside of this house." Without invitation, he dropped down onto one of the love seats. "But I was never invited."

"I guess there was just never an occasion." Self-consciously, Laura sat down on a chair, perching on the very edge of its cushioned seat, as though she might need to leave it in a hurry.

"Now, isn't that funny? I recall several occasions when I could have been invited."

She shot him a withering look. He just wasn't going to make this easy, was he? Did he want her to come right out and say that his kind wouldn't have been welcomed at any of the social events her family had hosted? She wouldn't be so gauche, no matter how severely she was provoked. Good manners were too deeply inbred.

"You were older. We had a different set of friends."

He found her tact amusing and laughed out loud. "We sure as hell did, Miss Laura." He cocked his head to one side and looked at her through narrowed eyes. "I *assume* it's still Miss Laura Nolan."

"Yes."

"How come?"

"I beg your pardon."

"How come it's still Miss?"

"I prefer to live as a single woman." Exuding disapproval of his ill-mannered question from every pore, she gave him a cool blue stare and tossed her hair back over her shoulders.

He leaned against the crewel-work pillows in the love seat, spread his arms along its back, and crossed one ankle over the other. "Well, now, Miss Laura," he drawled, "it's always been my contention that the only difference between 'a single woman' and an old maid is the number of lovers she has. How many have you got?"

Laura's face turned pink with fury. Her posture became even more erect, and she glared at him in what she hoped looked like open contempt, because that was exactly what she was feeling. "Enough."

"Anybody I know?"

"My social life is none of your business."

"Let's see, now." He glanced up at the ceiling and gave every impression that he was contemplating a problem. "To my recollection, the boys from this town fall into one of two categories. They either come back after college to run their daddies' businesses, or they leave and never come back, but move on to bigger and better things. And of the ones who have come back, I can't think of a bachelor among them. The way I hear it, they're all married and have a passel of kids." He looked at her goadingly. "Kinda makes me wonder where you're getting all your boyfriends."

Laura surged to her feet with every intention of dressing him down, putting him in his proper place, and demanding that he leave her house. But she saw the triumph glowing in his eyes and promptly dismissed that notion. She didn't want him to know that he had succeeded in baiting her.

Her lips were so stiff that they barely moved as she asked, "Would you care for something to drink while you're waiting?" She took a few steps toward the antique liquor cabinet. It was lined with lead-crystal decanters and priceless glassware.

"No, thank you."

His declination left her with nothing to do but return to her seat, feeling like a greater fool. Rigidly she sat there, trying to avoid watching him watching her. The silence stretched out. "Did you have an appointment with Mrs. Hightower?" He made a noncommittal sound that she took as affirmation. "Do you really want to buy this house?"

"It's for sale, isn't it?"

"Yes, it's for sale. It's just that . . . I mean . . ." She faltered when his stare became hard and cold. Nervously she wet her lips. "I can't imagine what's keeping Mrs. Hightower. She's usually so punctual."

"You haven't changed, Laura."

His use of her first name alone caused goose bumps to break out on her arms. No longer mocking, his voice was soft and raspy, the way she remembered it sounding when they had met on the street and he had spoken to her. She had always spoken back courteously, ducking her head modestly and hurrying on her way, in case anybody watching mistook her friendliness as a come-on.

For some reason, exchanging hellos with James Paden had always left her a trifle breathless and disconcerted. She had felt compromised just by his speaking her name, as though he had touched her instead. Maybe because his eyes *implied* more than a simple hello. But for whatever reason, she had always been affected.

She felt that same way now. Awkward. Tongue-tied. And guilty over nothing. "I'm older."

"You're better-looking."

"Thank you." She knotted her fingers together in her lap. Her palms were so sweaty, they made a damp spot on her skirt.

"Everything's still firm and compact." His eyes scaled down her with the practiced ease of a man who is accustomed to mentally undressing women. When he raised his eyes to her face again, he looked at her from beneath a shelf of brows.

"I try to watch my weight." She was uneasy at being scrutinized with such blatant sexual interest, but she couldn't quite bring herself to admonish him for it. It was safer to pretend she didn't notice.

"Your hair still looks shiny and soft. Remember

when I told you it was the color of a fawn?" Lying, she shook her head.

"You dropped your chemistry book in the hallway, and I picked it up for you. Your hair swung down across your cheek. That's when I told you it looked like a fawn."

It had been her algebra book and they were in the school cafeteria, not the hallway. She said nothing.

"It's still that same, soft color. And it still has those blond streaks around your face. Or do you have those put there now?"

"No, they're natural."

He smiled at her sudden response. Laura had the grace to smile back shyly. He stared at her for a long time. "As I said, you're the prettiest girl in town."

"The prettiest *rich* girl."

He shrugged. "Hell, everybody was rich compared to the Padens."

Laura glanced down at her hands, embarrassed for him. James had grown up on the wrong side of the tracks, literally. He had lived in a shack held together by whatever scrap materials his alcoholic father could salvage from the junkyard. From the outside the tiny house had looked like a patchwork quilt, a laughable eyesore. Laura had often wondered how James had managed to keep himself clean, living in that shack.

"I was sorry about your father," she said quietly. Old Hector Paden had died several years ago. His death went virtually unnoticed, certainly unlamented.

James laughed scoffingly. "Then you were the only one."

"How's your mother?"

He stood up suddenly, his body tense. "She's all right, I guess."

Laura was stunned by his apparent indifference. While James was growing up, Leona Paden had held countless jobs to support her son and husband. But because of chronic absenteeism and illness, she earned the reputation of being unreliable. Shortly after her husband's death, however, she had moved from the shack by the railroad tracks into a small, neat house in a respectable neighborhood. Laura rarely saw Mrs. Paden anymore. She kept to herself. It was rumored that James supported her, so it came as a shock to Laura now that he would dismiss his mother with an uncaring shrug.

He went around the room, picking up an object and examining it carefully before setting it down and going to the next. "Why are you selling the place?"

Laura didn't like feeling that he was a prosecutor cross-examining her, so she stood up, too, and went to the window with the hope that she would see Mrs. Hightower's car coming up the lane. "Father died last February, so I live here alone. It's ridiculous for one person to live in a house this large."

He watched her intently. She was careful to keep her expression inscrutable. "Before his death, only you and your father lived here?"

"Yes. Mother died a few years ago." She averted her eyes. "Of course Bo and Gladys Burton lived in the quarters," she added, referring to the couple who had worked as domestics for her family for as long as she could remember.

"They don't anymore?"

"No, I let them go."

"Why?"

"I didn't need them any longer."

"You don't need a housekeeper to help you take care of this rambling house? And didn't Bo do all the handiwork and yard work?"

"I like doing it all myself."

"Hmm."

That nonverbal observation clearly told her that he didn't believe her. His doubtfulness was highly irritating. "Look, Mr. Paden—"

"Oh, come on, Laura. I know it's been a long time since we've seen each other, but you can still call me James, for crying out loud."

"All right, James. It looks as though you and Mrs. Hightower got your signals crossed. Why don't you make another appointment to meet her here tomorrow?"

"I want to see the house tonight."

"I'm sorry. She's not here, and it doesn't look like she's coming."

"I waited a long time out there in the dark until you showed up. I really don't need the realtor, since you're here. You can show me around."

"I don't think that's proper."

One eyebrow inched its way up his forehead until it formed an inquisitive arch over his eye. "Why, Miss Laura, did you have something *im*proper in mind?"

"Of course not," she snapped. "I only meant that the house is Mrs. Hightower's listing. She asked me today if she could show a client the house this evening. I consented and promised to make myself scarce. The only reason I came home when I did was because I thought you'd be gone by now. I'm sure she wouldn't appreciate my interference."

"It makes no difference to me whether she appreciates it or not. *I'm* the client. The customer is always right, and I would welcome your interfer-

ence. Who could show the house better than someone who has lived in it since the day she was
born?"

The words went through Laura like vicious
shards of glass. Who indeed? Who knew and loved
every nook and cranny and creaky floorboard of the
house that had been built by her great-grand-
father? Who polished the heirloom silver, long
before it was necessary, just for the pleasure of
handling it? Who waxed the antique furniture
until it shone in the sunlight that filtered through
the windowpanes? Who knew a story behind
nearly every object in the house? Whose heart was
breaking because she was being forced to sell?

Laura Nolan.

For as long as she could remember, the house
and its history had entranced her. Her grandmother had told the stories that Laura, as a little
girl, had repeatedly requested and never tired of
hearing. Now Laura willed herself not to cry when
reminded that she would soon, by necessity, have
to part with the house.

"I might know more about the house than Mrs.
Hightower, but I still don't think it's a good idea for
me to butt in."

"Or is it the client that you don't think is a good
idea?"

She glanced up at him quickly. "I don't know
what you mean," she said hesitantly. He moved
forward, until he was standing so close to her, she
had to tilt her head back to look him in the face.

"You don't think I'm good enough to buy your
house."

Because he hit the target so squarely, Laura was
startled. "I think no such thing."

"Yes, you do. But no matter what you think of
me, my money's green and I can afford the house."

Feeling trapped, she moved away from him. "I've heard about your success with those . . . those . . ."

"Automotive-parts stores."

"I was very glad for you."

He laughed shortly, scornfully. "Yeah, I'm sure everybody in town has toasted my success. They were so sure when I left here ten years ago that I'd be in prison by now."

"Well, what did you expect everybody to think? The way you—Never mind."

"No, go on," he said, stepping around in front of her again. "Tell me. The way I what?"

"The way you caroused in those cars you were always tinkering with."

"I worked in a garage. Tinkering with cars was how I made my living."

"But you delighted in scaring other drivers by whipping in and out of traffic with your hot rods and motorcycles. That's how you got your kicks. Just like tonight!" she said, pointing toward the lawn through the wide, tall windows. "Why were you hiding there in the bushes just waiting to scare me to death?"

He grinned. "I wasn't waiting for you. I was waiting for Mrs. Hightower."

"Well, you would have scared her too. Looming out of the dark on that horrible, noisy thing. She would have fainted. You should be ashamed of yourself."

He leaned down, laughing softly. "You can still get mad as the dickens, can't you, Laura?"

She drew herself up. "I'm extremely even-tempered."

He laughed again. "I remember when you lit into Joe Don Perkins for knocking over your cherry Coke at the soda fountain in the drugstore. A bunch of us had gone in there to buy . . . uh . . . never mind what we were buying, but I'll never forget how Joe Don tucked in his tail and slunk out of the drugstore after you let him have it with both barrels. You called him a big, clumsy oaf."

James was bending over her now, having backed her against the windowsill. He reached up and playfully tugged on a strand of light blond hair that lay against her cheek, then rested his palm there. "I remember thinking how damned exciting you were when you got mad." His voice dropped. "You're still exciting." He stroked her cheek.

"Don't," she said sharply, turning her head away.

The sensual smile on his lips narrowed into a line of bitterness. He withdrew his hand. "You don't want me to touch you? Why? Aren't these hands clean enough?" He held both hands, fingers spread wide, inches in front of her face. "Look, Laura. I don't work in a garage anymore repairing rich folks' cars. See? There's no grease under my fingernails now."

"I didn't mean—"

"The hell you didn't. But let me tell you something. I'm clean enough now to breach the door of Twenty-two Indigo Place and I'm clean enough to touch you."

His breath struck her lips in hot gusts. She gazed up at him with fearful blue eyes. He took another step closer.

They were suddenly caught in the headlights of a car as it pulled into the driveway that formed a half circle in front of the house. Laura's instinct was to duck for cover and put as much distance as possible between James Paden and herself.

But she couldn't move until he got out of her way, and he didn't move for what seemed like a long time. And for as long as he took to straighten up to his full height again and move away, he kept his eyes riveted on her face.

Flustered, she smoothed her hair and ran her damp hands down her skirt before making her way to the front door to answer Mrs. Hightower's knock.

"Hello, dear." The real estate agent—round, jolly and friendly—blustered in. "I'm sorry I'm late, but I was unavoidably detained. I tried to call . . . Oh, hello! You must be Mr. Paden." She advanced on him like a Sherman tank, her hand extended. She shook his heartily. "I apologize again for being late. Isn't it lucky that you caught Laura at home? I should have been here to introduce you, but then, you mentioned on the telephone that you already know her, didn't you?"

"Yes," he said in a low, thrumming voice. "We've known each other for years." Laura avoided looking at him.

"And have you seen the house?"

"We were waiting for you," he said.

"Well, then, I won't delay you from seeing it any longer. It's so lovely. Laura, you have such insight into the house's history. Will you accompany us, please?"

"I'd be happy to," Laura said, ignoring James's I-told-you-so expression.

For the next half hour, they toured the gracious rooms of 22 Indigo Place. Though the house had been in Laura's family for several generations, it had been carefully and lovingly maintained. There were certain areas that needed attention, but by and large the house was immaculate. There was a total of fourteen rooms, exclusive of the entrance hall and the central hallway upstairs. Each room was beautifully furnished in keeping with the Greek revival architecture.

Laura tried to sound detached as she went through her spiel, but, as always when talking about Indigo Place, she quickly warmed to her subject. Her audience was attentive. James was charming and polite to the realtor, who basked in his attention. Laura gritted her teeth each time Mrs. Hightower simpered at something clever he said.

They concluded the tour in the entrance hall. Mrs. Hightower smiled up at James. "Isn't it wonderful, Mr. Paden? Was I exaggerating over the phone?"

"No, you weren't, Mrs. Hightower, but then, I was acquainted with this address. I've always admired the house from afar." Laura took the barb for what it was, but ignored the significant glance he cast in her direction. "I'll give it careful consideration tonight."

"Very well. Please call me if you have any questions." The realtor turned to Laura. "Thank you for letting us see the house tonight. As soon as I hear from Mr. Paden, I'll be in touch with you."

"Thank you, Mrs. Hightower."

"Good night, Laura." Laura looked down at the hand that was extended to her. It *was* clean. And tanned. And strong. A well-shaped, masculine hand that she thought was probably capable of exerting tremendous force and giving a woman exquisite pleasure.

"Good night, James." She clasped his attractive hand briefly before letting it go. "Welcome back to Gregory."

He smiled at her in a way that said he knew he was about as welcome in Gregory as a skunk at a flower show.

He left with Mrs. Hightower, and Laura closed the door behind them. Even through the heavy door, she could hear the realtor chattering in praise of the house. She was treating this prospective buyer with kid gloves. Property that commanded a price as high as that of 22 Indigo Place was restricted to all but a handful of buyers. Thus far no one had seriously looked at the property. James Paden was the first real candidate for new ownership, and Mrs. Hightower didn't want to lose the potential sale.

Laura didn't move from the front door until she heard the motorcycle follow Mrs. Hightower's car out of the driveway. As she went through the rooms turning out lights, she chastised herself for not asking Mrs. Hightower who her client was when she called earlier that afternoon. The only thing she had told Laura was that he was an Atlanta millionaire who was looking for a home in which to spend his early retirement.

Laura had expected a much older man. She had expected a stranger. She would never have expected James Paden.

Scattered throughout the last few years, there had been numerous accounts of him in the local newspaper. Only a few years after he left Gregory, he had earned himself a name driving race cars. For fans of that sport, he was a celebrity, having set impressive records for speed and daring while still in his twenties. There had been an extensive write-up in an Atlanta newspaper about his retirement from the race track. A few months later Laura read that he had opened an automotive-parts store.

Since then, the townspeople of Gregory had watched with growing interest as their hometown boy built that first store into a phenomenally successful chain. The most recent report of James Paden—whom up to that point none of Gregory's citizens had wanted to claim—was that he had sold the chain of stores to a conglomerate for a staggering amount of money.

Laura didn't care how much money he had made or how successful he had become, he was still uncouth and ill-mannered. And how typically lower class it was of him to flaunt his success in the face of a town that had openly scorned him.

Who cared?

She certainly didn't. Why couldn't he have been satisfied to keep his millions in Atlanta? They didn't need them in Gregory.

Unfortunately that wasn't quite true. She needed money desperately.

The weight of her problem settled over her like a suit of chain mail. It stayed with her as she went upstairs and entered her bedroom, which, she thought thankfully, James had given no more than a cursory glance when he had viewed the house.

As she undressed, Laura bitterly recalled the day the executor of her father's estate had asked her to come to see him. In his impressive book-lined office he'd delivered the devastating news that she had been bequeathed nothing but a list of irate creditors.

Aghast, she had listened as he explained that her father had been a disastrous financial manager and had squandered the family fortune on bad investments and unsound speculations. The attorney had put it to her kindly, but bluntly. She was broke, having absolutely no means with which to pay the accumulated bills.

"But we lived—"

"Very well. Randolph would never admit that he

was in trouble, much less let you or your mother know that you were headed for financial disaster."

Laura had scanned the ledger sheets until the enormity of her difficulties overwhelmed her. "I can't even afford to eat."

"I'm sorry, Laura, that this is your inheritance."

"At least I have Indigo Place," she had said reflectively, flipping through a stack of bills. The attorney's heavy sigh brought her head up, and she gazed at him with mounting dread. "I *do* still have Indigo Place, don't I?"

He covered her hand with his. "It's mortgaged to the hilt, my dear. The bank has notified me that unless they can recoup their losses within six months, they will have no choice but to foreclose. I strongly suggest that you sell."

That had been the final blow. She had lain her head on the attorney's desk and sobbed. Slowly, however, she had confronted the reality of her dilemma. That she was penniless was untenable, but nonetheless true.

As quietly as possible she had put 22 Indigo Place up for sale. When word got around, as she knew it would, she had squelched negative gossip by saying that she was tired of having to maintain the house, that she hated being shackled to it, that she wanted the freedom to travel without being liable for the upkeep of the property.

She would travel, all right, straight out of town to find herself a job as soon as the property was sold.

She got into bed and switched out the light, staring, as she always had, at the magnolia tree outside her second-story window. Time was running out. She barely had a month before the bank's deadline. Declaring bankruptcy and having everyone in town know about her father's failure was unthinkable. Above all else, she didn't want her family's sterling reputation scandalized. She must sell the house, and soon.

But she'd be damned before she'd let a reprobate like James Paden move into it!

Two

Laura woke up late and groggily, not having slept well after it had taken hours for her to fall asleep in the first place. She sensed that she had had a disturbing dream, too, but didn't want to recall it. Instinctively she knew that she didn't want to know what—or rather *whom*—the dream had been about.

Waking up with pessimistic doldrums wasn't something new to her. Through her father's lengthy illness, his death, and the discovery of her financial dilemma, Laura had kept up a brave front, but she scarcely remembered what it was like to look forward to getting up in the morning. Recently, new days only promised new problems.

She trudged into the bathroom adjoining her bedroom and took a shower, first scalding, then as cold as she could stand it, in an effort to perk herself up. Unhappiness made her lethargic, but the shower remedied it somewhat.

She pulled on an old pair of denim cut-offs and a T-shirt with "So Many Men, So Little Time" printed on it. The T-shirt had been a gag gift from a friend, who had picked it up on a trip to New Orleans. Barefoot, with her hair still wrapped in a towel, she went downstairs to brew a pot of coffee, which she needed badly.

The sound of the doorbell roused her out of the trance the dripping coffee maker had induced. Her feet barely sounded on the hardwood floors and antique Persian rugs as she made her way to the front door. When she peeped through the dining-room drapes to see who the early caller was, she squeezed her eyes shut, clenched her fists, and cursed beneath her breath.

Hazarding one glance in the entrance-hall mirror, she groaned and wished she hadn't even looked. No makeup, barefoot, wet hair wrapped in a towel. Great. Terrific.

And, dammit, he looked gorgeous.

She pulled the door open, but said nothing, only greeted him with a look as sour as her mood.

He took in her attire and had the unforgivable audacity to laugh. "G'morning."

"Hello."

She had to stand there and watch him as he read the slogan on her T-shirt. Then she had to endure his smirk, which was skeptical. She wanted to slap it right off his face. Instead, she kept her expression blasé and bored.

Glancing past his impressive pair of shoulders, she saw that he had traded the motorcycle in favor of a silver sports car, the make of which she didn't even recognize. It was so low and sleek, she wondered how he had folded his long frame into it.

"Are you going to invite me in?"

"No."

"*May* I come in?"

"What for?"

"Didn't Mrs. Hightower call?"

"No."

Even as she spoke the word aloud, the telephone rang. He winked. "Bet that's her now." Laura only glared up at him, her body still acting as a barrier at the door. "I suggest you answer the phone," he said after several strident rings had failed to budge her.

Maintaining her poise despite her dishabille, Laura turned her back on him and went to the telephone, tucked into a nook beneath the stairs.

"Hello . . . Oh, good morning, Mrs. Hightower." She looked at James, who was coming through the front door uninvited. As he closed the door behind him, he returned her look and grinned complacently. "He's already here," Laura said crossly. "I wish you had . . . Oh, you did? . . . I guess I was in the shower . . . Well . . . I really . . ." She sighed heavily, then said, "All right . . . Yes, I'm sure. No bother. Good-bye."

She replaced the receiver in the cradle and slowly turned to face her unwelcome guest. "She said you wanted to see the house again. Why? You saw it last night."

"If I decide to buy it, I'll be making quite an investment. Don't you think I should view it in the daylight?"

"I suppose so." Lord, she wished she didn't look so wretched. She wished her T-shirt weren't so old and soft and clingy. She wished she had worn a bra this morning. In fact, with his eyes moving over her, she wished she were dressed in a long, dark shroud from chin to toes. Her legs felt more naked than they had ever felt. Even her feet felt vulnerable when he glanced down at them.

"Well," she said, edging her way toward the dining room, "make yourself at home. I was just brewing coffee—"

"Thanks, I'd love some."

Her mouth fell open slightly as she stared at him. She hadn't invited him to have coffee with her. James Paden had absolutely no manners. Any other man would sense her embarrassment and go about his business as unobtrusively as possible. She should have known not to expect that kind of consideration from him.

"In the kitchen," she said ungraciously.

"Fine. I need to see it again anyway."

He followed her through the formal dining room and into the sunny kitchen. The aroma of fresh coffee greeted them. "Won't you sit down?" Her lips fashioned a stiff smile, but she made the invitation sound discouraging.

"In a minute," he said absently. He was assessing the kitchen with the thoroughness of a master chef. "Will all the appliances stay?"

"I hadn't thought about it." She reached overhead into the cabinet for cups and saucers and became aware of several things at once: how the reaching motion stretched the T-shirt even more tightly across her breasts, how short and snug the cut-offs actually were, and how good James Paden smelled. His skin smelled of soap and spicy aftershave. His mouth would taste like peppermint.

Heaven forbid that she should ever have an occasion to taste it, but—

"Well?"

"Well, what?" She did her best to fill two coffee cups, though her hands were shaking. Always before she had cursed this kitchen for being so large that it required unnecessary steps to reach things. In the last few minutes it seemed to have shrunk drastically.

"The appliances. Thanks," he said, taking one of the cups and saucers from her hand.

"Oh, well, I guess they stay. They've been here since the kitchen was remodeled and modernized. I certainly won't have much use for them and they probably wouldn't bring much if I tried to sell them. Cream or sugar?"

"No, thanks." He sipped his coffee. "Where are you going?"

Her eyes followed the trail of steam rising out of her coffee cup. Eventually they clashed with his. "Going? When?"

"When you sell the house?"

"Somewhere else," she answered obliquely.

They studied each other for several seconds. Laura was the first to look away. "As you can see, all the appliances are in good condition and perfect working order."

He went over everything with a fine-tooth comb. Laura much preferred his looking at her house and its furnishings to his looking at her, but his meticulousness was unnerving and aggravating. He found a knick in the tile grouting and picked at it with his index fingernail.

"That's just loose grouting," she said impatiently.

"I know. I could fix that myself." He looked down at her breasts, making no attempt to hide his fascination. His gaze stayed fixed there for a long time before crawling back up to her face. "I'm very good with my hands."

She was held captivated by his steady green stare for the length of several heartbeats, then she turned away angrily. *I'll just bet you are*, she thought scathingly.

Even though it burned her tongue, she finished her coffee in one huge swallow and set her cup and saucer on the counter top with a solid thump. She didn't want him here. He unsettled her and made her nervous and defensive. But she couldn't just throw him out. He was Mrs. Hightower's client. The only choice Laura had was to conclude their business as soon as possible.

"What would you like to see?"

Crossing his ankles, he propped his hips against the counter and leisurely sipped his coffee, all the while keeping his eyes on her. "I haven't seen much so far. What do you feel like showing me?"

The double-entendre didn't escape her, but she ignored it. Didn't he ever think of anything else? His reputation as a womanizer wasn't an exaggeration. If all that was said about him was true, it was a miracle to Laura that he could get his pants zipped.

And with that thought, her eyes moved down to check it out. Which was a mistake. Because his jeans fit. Well. Very well. And though they were properly zipped, they couldn't camouflage his gender. If that bulge behind his fly weren't enough to convince her that this person was all man, consummately male, then the hard, trim thighs that framed his sex would have.

No paunchy torso this. Oh, no. His casual shirt didn't even wrinkle over the flat plane of his stomach, but it was stretched somewhat to accommodate his chest. She pretended, even to herself, that she didn't see that intriguing crop of gold-tipped brown hair in the V of his shirt.

Nevertheless, after her survey of him, she was powerless to speak, and it was he who broke the silence. "What about the cellar?"

"What about it?"

"You mentioned it last night, but I didn't see it. Does this door lead down to it?"

He went to the door across the kitchen and tried

to open it. "The key is hanging there on a nail," Laura informed him, forcing her feet to move over the tile floor. She had to stand close to him to reach the key, which was hidden between the refrigerator and the wall.

"Do you always keep it locked?"

"Yes."

"Why? Is this the closet with all the family skeletons?"

She gave him a dirty look over her shoulder as she unlocked the door. "No, but this is the only part of Indigo Place I've never liked."

"Why?"

"I don't know," she said shrugging. "It's spooky."

"Then maybe I'd better go first."

He wedged past her. She flattened herself as best she could against the doorjamb, but he touched her anyway. Everywhere and all at once. His front dragged across hers. Her entire body surged to life, as though she'd just been plugged into an electrical socket. She wouldn't have been surprised to see sparks fly.

On the second step down, he turned back. "Are you coming?"

She had heard that leading line in a movie once, and the heroine had supplied an equally glib and suggestive response. All Laura could do was curse herself for thinking along those channels and stammer, "Uh, no, you go ahead. I think I'll have another cup of coffee while you explore."

"Please. It is kinda spooky. Besides, I need you to show me around. What if I get lost? And if I have a question—"

"Oh, all right," Laura said irritably. She tentatively laid her bare foot on the wooden step.

"Here, let me help you."

Before she realized what he was going to do, he

had clasped her hand warmly in his. Slowly he led her down the dark steps. "Watch your step," he cautioned.

"There's a light switch on your right at the bottom," she said, her voice echoing eerily off the walls. He found it and switched it. Nothing happened. "Sorry. I guess the bulb is burned out."

"That's okay. With the door open I can see well enough."

She had hoped that without the light he would have called a halt to the tour of the cellar. She had even made a partial turn back up the stairs, but he had kept her hand firmly imprisoned in his. Now she had no choice but to follow him as he stepped into the underground room.

The floor was damp on her bare feet. The cellar smelled like freshly turned dirt. It was musty. She envisioned spiders and mice and all things unpleasant.

"What's in all those jars on the shelves?"

"Preserves and jams. Canned fruits and vegetables. Gladys put them up before she left."

"Are they any good?"

"They're delicious. She's a wonderful cook."

"Pity you had to let her go."

Laura was instantly defensive. "I didn't *have* to. I chose to."

He didn't comment, but asked another question, then another, until his curiosity about the cellar was satisfied. He had held her hand the whole while, but she didn't realize how hard she'd been gripping his until they headed back toward the stairs. Light spilled onto them from the kitchen door overhead. She eased her grip considerably.

"You really don't like this cellar, do you?" he asked softly, pausing at the bottom step.

"No, I don't."

"And you're cold."

He began rubbing her upper arms vigorously. For a moment Laura was stunned by his touch. She just stood there and let his hands briskly slide from her elbows to her shoulders and back, again and again, until she began to warm. Or did her returning warmth stem from embarrassment? Because James wasn't looking at her face, or even at her chill-bumped arms. He was looking at her breasts. That was how he had known she was cold.

Swiftly she threw off his hands and clambered up the steps. "I think I need another cup of coffee." As soon as she cleared the door, she rushed to retrieve her cup and pour more coffee into it. "How about you?"

"I'm fine, thanks." He methodically relocked the cellar door and returned the key to its hiding place. "But I think I know something that would make you feel a whole lot better than coffee ever could."

She came around slowly, and just as slowly lowered the coffee cup from her lips. His voice was low and deep. It hinted that there was a high level of intimacy between them. His eyes were suggestive, his walk self-assured, as he moved toward her. Knowing she should run, Laura couldn't move. Not even when he raised his hands and reached for her.

Slowly he worked the knot out of the towel wrapped around her head and removed it. Her wet hair tumbled around her face and fell to her shoulders. Dropping the towel, James raised both hands again, plowed his fingers through her hair, and raked it away from her face. He dragged his fingers through the damp strands, pushing against the tangles until they worked free. When he had combed through to the silky ends several times, he closed his hands around her throat and massaged the vertebrae in the back of her neck with his fingertips.

"Now, didn't that help relieve some of the tension in your neck?"

It certainly had. It had also robbed her knees of the strength to support her. It had also built a fire deep in her belly. It was spreading heat through her middle and melting her thighs.

"Yes, thank you." Her primary goal now was to escape him before falling victim to his undeniable charm. She shook off his hands and forced herself to step around him. Somehow she managed to set her cup and saucer on the table before she dropped them. "Why . . . why don't we go through the rooms downstairs first? Then if there's anything else you want to see, I'll show you."

"All right. Lead the way."

Having the towel off her head did nothing to restore her confidence. Wet hair fresh from a shampoo seemed far too personal. She felt exposed and violated each time he looked at her, but she relied on her inbred composure to get her through a tour of the lower floor.

Of course, this was all a charade. She wasn't going to accept a contract on the house from James Paden if he trebled her asking price. It almost seemed profane for him to be moving through the rooms. She shuddered to think of him and his rowdy friends storming through her house the way they had the movie theater on Saturday nights, causing a ruckus until the manager threw them out.

That would only happen over her dead body.

"This is Father's office," she said, leading him into a spacious, paneled room at the back of the house. It was furnished in leather and heavy oak and still smelled like pipe tobacco. A bear rug sprawled on the floor in front of the fireplace, and several hunting trophies mutely snarled at them from above the mantel. An antique billiard table with old-fashioned leather pouches dominated the center of the room.

"He played pool?" James asked.

"By the hour," she said, laughing at fond memories.

"So that's the difference."

Surprised by his sneering tone, she turned. "The difference?"

"Between a gentleman and a ne'er-do-well. If you hang out in the pool hall you're labeled trash, but if you shoot billiards by the hour in your own house, you're a gentleman." He cast another bitter glance at the pool table, then at her, and said harshly, "Let's go upstairs."

She didn't like the underlying sinister tone of his voice. It was bad enough to lead a man, especially a man with James Paden's reputation, up the stairs toward the bedrooms of an otherwise empty house. But when his "Let's go upstairs" carried with it the veiled threat that once there he might exact punishment from her for all the disparagement he had suffered, the sinking sensation in the pit of her stomach intensified.

However, by the time they reached the second floor, his stern expression had relaxed. Laura showed him the master suite first, thinking that might appease him. But when they left it, he merely stood in the hallway, looking at her inquiringly, until she showed him the other two bedrooms, which shared a bathroom. She then made a beeline for the top of the stairs. "Now I'll show you—"

"What's that?"

Without even turning, she knew what he was

referring to. Sure enough, he was indicating the corner bedroom. "That's my bedroom," she answered reluctantly.

"May I see it?"

"Is it necessary?"

"I think it is."

Why wasn't Mrs. Hightower here doing her job, earning her six-percent commission? Laura berated herself for agreeing to show him around without the realtor. The woman's effusiveness was irritating, but her presence sanctioned James Paden's being under her roof asking to see her bedroom.

"I'm sure that if you make a serious offer, Mrs. Hightower will schedule—"

"But I'm here now."

He slid his hands deep into his pockets, cocked his head to one side, and looked for all the world as if he would stand there until Doomsday or until he got his way, whichever came first. Such insolence was insufferable, but, short of engaging in an argument that in the long run would only postpone his leaving, Laura conceded the point.

"All right." Making no effort to mask her hostility, she led him back down the hall and stepped aside to let him pass through the door. His eyes immediately homed in on the bed, which she hadn't had the energy to make when she first got up. The pillow bore the distinct impression of her head. The pastel sheets were rumpled. The bed looked comfy and inviting. It looked wanton.

He walked straight to it and sat down. He ran his hands over the sheet beneath him. "I always wondered what Laura Nolan's bed looked like."

She was tempted to quip something like, "If I weren't flat broke, you'd die wondering," but she didn't. Instead she said, "I'm sorry it's not made. I didn't have time this morning."

"That's okay. I prefer my beds unmade."

She swallowed, pushing down the thrill she experienced at seeing his hands caressing her bed sheets.

After giving her a look that fairly steamed, he left the bed and crossed to her dressing table. He took inventory of her perfume atomizers, the string of pearls she had forgotten to replace in its velvet box, her collection of antique hatpins, and the crystal ring box her grandmother had given her.

The chaise longue in the corner of the room caught his eye. He looked at it for a long moment, before glancing back at her with a hint of a smile. She got the feeling that he was thinking of something extremely dirty.

He went to the wide windows and gazed out for a long time, his back to her. Her bedroom overlooked the sweeping backyard of the property, the fishing pier, the boathouse, and the waters of St. Gregory's Sound beyond. "Nice view."

"I've always loved it."

"Has this always been your bedroom?"

"Except for the four years when I went to college."

He pivoted on his heels. "This is where you slept when I first knew you?"

She nodded.

"You always looked so . . . perfect. Untouchable. Like a doll. This is like a doll's room." He glanced at the bed again. "Do you always sleep alone?"

Her chin went up a fraction. "None of your business."

He grinned. "I meant no kitty cat, no puppy dog, no teddy bear?"

"No," she said stiffly, crossing her arms over her

middle, then wishing she hadn't because the gesture only drew his gaze down to her breasts.

"I like this room. It's cozy. Intimate." She held her ground, even though her cheeks were flaming and her heart was pounding. His words sounded innocent enough, but she knew they were calculated to sound suggestive. She wanted to run from the room, to cover her breasts, which were betraying her by responding to the evocative mood he was creating. "Is that the bathroom?"

"Yes."

He went to the partially opened door and stepped inside. Laura didn't dare follow him in. Standing in her bedroom with him had been bad enough. She wouldn't subject herself to further embarrassment.

A few moments later, he came out. "These were hanging on the shower curtain rod. They're dry."

Her face went white with dismay to see a pair of her stockings, a bra, and a pair of panties lying in the palm of his extended hand. "Th—thank you," she said ludicrously, reaching for the frilly undergarments. They had known his touch. The silk was still warm from his hand. She dropped the lingerie onto a chair as though it were condemning evidence of some sordid crime.

"Well, I think that's all for now," he said.

She followed him from the room, still too shocked and embarrassed to speak, hardly able to move. He waited for her to catch up with him at the bottom of the stairs, then let her escort him to the front door. "You'll be hearing from me or Mrs. Hightower."

"All right."

Other than to make him angry, it would serve no purpose at this point to tell him that she wouldn't accept his offer on the house no matter how attractive it was. Actually, she doubted that he was seriously considering buying the estate. Why would a man of his means, a free-spirited swinger like him, want to saddle himself with the responsibility of owning an historical house?

His reason for wanting to see the house in the first place was probably nothing more than perverse curiosity. He'd never been invited into it before. Now, because he had money and celebrity, he could come and go as he pleased without feeling the bite of class restriction. No doubt he enjoyed riding roughshod over everybody, since the tables were turned. Because he had never been invited to Indigo Place, he had come to rub her nose in his success.

Thinking along those lines, Laura said snidely, "I hope you got what you came here for."

She regretted the words the moment they left her mouth, particularly when he halted on his way out the door and slowly turned around. He no longer looked like a thirty-year-old millionaire. He was eighteen again, wild and undisciplined and dangerous. A rebellious lock of hair had fallen over his brow. That sardonic curl of his lips, which passed for a smile, was as familiar to her now as it had been so long ago on the pages of the high school yearbook.

He closed the door he had just opened and said, "Not quite."

With one lithe movement he grasped her upper arms, turned her around, and pressed her against the door. Splaying his hands wide on either side of her head, he leaned down and forward, at the same time wedging her thighs apart with his knee.

His mouth swooped down on hers. She dodged it, slinging her head from side to side. "No. No!"

But he was relentless and persistent and,

though he wasn't even using his hands, the moment his mouth captured hers in a fiercely hot, open-mouthed kiss, she was defeated. He applied just the right amount of suction. His tongue exercised the perfect blend of command and caress. The very heat of his kiss melted her last gasp of resistance.

It was one of those ravenous kisses she thought only existed in movies. He was hungry, and feasted on her mouth as if it were a rich, delicious dessert. He came back for sample after sample, tasting her. Through it all, his thigh was gently sawing between hers.

When at last he lifted his head, her lips were left rosy and dewy, her eyes limpid, her body warm and malleable. Her breasts rose and fell quickly. He lowered his gaze to them, brazenly touched the raised center of one, and made it harder with three lazy circles of his thumb. "Oh, baby, you're good," he murmured. Then he groaned and kissed her again.

Laura was humiliated by the liberty he took with her, even more so by her acquiescence to it. She succeeded in working herself free and shoved him away. Breathlessly she faced him, her whole body rigid with rage. "Why did you do that?"

She had been shaken to the core, but he seemed merely amused by her anger. "I just thought you needed a good kissing."

Before she could offer a suitably scathing comeback, he was gone.

"I don't understand, Laura."

Laura, rubbing her forehead in the vain hope of relieving her pounding headache, held the telephone receiver to her ear. She had dreaded getting this call from Mrs. Hightower. It was proving to be as difficult as she had imagined.

"I'm sorry to disappoint you, but the contract isn't acceptable." She could imagine the real estate agent on the other end of the line slowly counting to ten.

"But he's offering exactly what you're asking!" she exclaimed. "Down to the last decimal point."

"I know, I know," Laura said, gnawing her lower lip. "It's not the money."

"Have you had second thoughts about selling?"

"Of course not." The realtor's question was academic, because she knew the necessity behind the sale of 22 Indigo Place.

"Well, then?"

Laura squirmed in her chair. "It's not the money. It's the buyer," she said softly.

"I see."

"I don't think you do, Mrs. Hightower. Please don't think I'm a snob. You must understand that this house has always belonged to my family. To me it's not just a piece of property. In terms of what it means to me, its value can't be measured in dollars and cents. A lot of responsibility goes with owning an estate like this. I want to make certain that the person who buys it takes that into account."

"I doubt Mr. Paden would be a neglectful owner. He has the reputation of being an astute businessman."

And a ladies' man, Laura thought bitterly. She was still disgusted with herself for what had happened earlier that day. How could she have stood there and let him use her like that?

She had been several classes behind James in school, but she and every other girl in Gregory High School had known about James Paden's kissing talents. Girls who succumbed to it were wont to brag. They were secretly envied, but forever branded "bad," and were given wide berth by any girl who valued her reputation. So what did that make Laura Nolan now? She hadn't only succumbed, she had participated.

"I'm not talking about business acumen," she snapped, taking out her impatience with herself on the realtor. In a much more conciliatory tone she said, "I'm talking about feelings. Attachments. A sense of permanence. I'm sorry, Mrs. Hightower, but I don't think James Paden is the buyer I want to sell to."

"I was under the impression you were desperate," she said frostily.

"I am," Laura returned in just as chilly a voice. "But if you don't respect the heritage of the property as I do, there are other—"

"I apologize," Mrs. Hightower rushed to say. "Of course I understand your sentimental attachment to the house. It's just unfortunate at this point that we have to be so discriminating. What am I supposed to tell Mr. Paden?"

"Tell him that I said no to his offer."

"He's not an easy man to say no to."

That was an understatement. "Do your best."

"Very well," Mrs. Hightower said dispiritedly.

Laura regretted the difficulty she was causing the realtor, but felt strongly about her conviction. James Paden would never have her house if she could help it.

But as Mrs. Hightower predicted, he didn't take Laura's refusal lying down. The realtor called back twice that same afternoon with amendments to the original contract. Though James had sweetened the pot considerably both times, Laura stubbornly refused the offers. Finally, weary of his doggedness and the realtor's subtle reproach, she left the house to keep from answering the telephone again.

It was Friday afternoon, and the streets of town were thronged with preweekend shoppers, workers chasing to the bank to have their paychecks cashed, and young people getting a head start on "cruising the main drag," which was one of the prime forms of recreation in a town as small as Gregory.

Thanks to a sultry breeze off the sound, the air was humid. Laura dreaded the thought of eating anything hot for dinner, so she stopped at a fresh-produce stand to pick up the makings of a fruit salad.

She was selecting the most succulent of Georgia peaches when a car slid to a stop close behind her. The passenger door swung open, nearly catching her on the backs of her calves. She turned around and met James Paden's brooding stare as he leaned out the car door.

"Get in."

Three

She ignored him, turning her back.

"I said to get in."

She continued to give the peaches her undivided attention.

"I don't mind making scenes, Laura, as I'm sure you know. But I don't think you'd like it much if I caught you by the hair and hauled you in. Now, unless you want to give the good folks of Gregory something juicy to discuss over supper tonight, you'd better get your sweet tush in this damn car."

His voice was soft and low, but carried with it a very real threat that Laura thought she'd be wise to heed. So far, no one had noticed that he was speaking to her, but he could change that in an instant. On top of all her other problems, the last thing she needed was to have her name linked to his. He might be wealthier, but he was still disreputable. The people of Gregory had long memories.

In his present frame of mind, it would be less chancy to go with him while he remained undetected than it would be to risk his carrying out his threat and make a scene.

"I'll be back later, Mr. Potee," Laura called to the proprietor of the produce market. He was busy with another customer and only gave her a cursory nod.

She got into the passenger seat of the sports car and closed the door hurriedly. James shoved the car into first gear and it took off like a rocket, burying Laura in the cushiony leather seat, in which she was very nearly reclining already.

He drove fast but skillfully. Even so, Laura held her breath at the lightning speed with which he negotiated the streets of town, until they were outside the city limits and on the straightaway.

"Are you going to tell me where we're going?" she asked his profile.

If he was angry, he gave no indication of it. He was practically reclining in his seat too. When he wasn't shifting gears, his right wrist was draped over the padded leather steering wheel. His left elbow was crooked in the open window. He seemed not to notice that the wind was tearing through his hair, much less that it was wreaking havoc on Laura's. He glanced at her briefly before answering, "Parking."

"Pa—" She couldn't even fashion the word. Her mouth had suddenly gone dry. She turned her head and stared out the windshield. The road he had taken east led to the shore of St. Gregory's Sound. In the distance, she could see the water through the trees.

The road narrowed, and finally came to a dead end on the marshy beach of a cove. James cut the powerful engine. They were in a deserted area, and the surrounding trees seemed to close in on them ominously. Dense vines wound themselves around the branches of the trees and draped to the ground. Pines reached for heaven.

The beach itself was only a narrow strip of sand and was littered with clumps of sawgrass. In the twilight, night birds were just beginning to gather in small choirs. Insects buzzed low over the sluggish water lapping at the shoreline.

Reflexively Laura jumped when James stretched his arm across the back of her seat. "Relax."

"I'll bet you say that to all the girls you bring here," she responded tartly, shrinking against her door.

He laughed, a deep, seductive sound. "Come to think of it, I did."

"And did they? Relax, I mean."

His eyes looked lazy and slumberous when they lowered to her mouth. "Most of them."

"And the others?"

"The others were too excited to relax."

"Excited?"

"Sexually excited."

You had to ask, didn't you, dummy?

"And just plain excited to be here with me."

His conceit was beyond belief, and she made a scoffing sound. "Well, I'm neither relaxed nor excited. I'm mad as hell. Will you please take me back to the market so I can get my car and go home?"

"No. Not yet. We're going to have a little chat first."

"We could have had a little chat over the telephone. But then, that would have been proper and conventional, wouldn't it? And you've never done a proper or conventional thing in your life."

"Right." Smiling, he leaned closer. "And you know what? I think you like that about me. I think you like it a lot. That's why your heart is beating as fast as a frightened bunny's."

She didn't want to honor his observation with an argument, mainly because he was right on both accounts, and secondly because the only way he could have known her heart was beating so fast was by looking at the cloth vibrating over it. For safety's sake, she merely returned her stony gaze out the front windshield.

"Why didn't you accept the offer I made on your house?"

"It was unacceptable."

"I offered what you were asking."

"I want more than money from the party who buys Indigo Place."

"Like what?"

"Like commitment."

"Care to expound?"

"I don't want some fly-by-night character to come in and buy it, then let it go to ruin."

"I don't intend to do that."

"I'm sure you'd tire of it soon. It's too isolated. Gregory doesn't have the kind of glittering night life that I feel certain you're accustomed to. You'd get bored with the town and the responsibility that goes with maintaining an estate like Indigo Place."

"I want to retire there."

"Retire?" she asked with open skepticism. "At thirty-two?"

"Yes, retire," he said with a smile that crept over his mouth gradually. "Until I can think of an interesting way to make my next million."

No one with any integrity talked openly about his financial success. His comment only confirmed how uncouth he was. But if he could be blunt, then so could she. "I don't want to sell the house to you. Period."

"There are laws against discrimination," he replied calmly.

"I'll think of some way around them."

"I can afford the property."

"I know. But Indigo Place isn't a trophy you've earned for a job well done."

"Meaning what?" Defensively his body tensed, and Laura knew she had struck a nerve.

"Meaning that you don't crave the property nearly as much as you crave the respectability synonymous with the address. What you don't seem to realize is that honor and nobility aren't for sale. Respect is something even your millions can't buy you, Mr. Paden."

His jaw bunched with anger, but he didn't contradict her. Finally he said, "All right, you see through me. But you're as transparent as glass yourself. I know the real reason you don't want to sell to me."

"And what might that real reason be?" she asked sweetly.

Her coyness provoked his temper. He snatched her upper arm so quickly, she jumped in fear. "My money's not good enough, that's why."

"That's not—"

"Hear me out. My money isn't 'old money.' It hasn't molded in bank vaults through generations of gentility. It was earned, not by tilling this precious lowland, but by selling a product. To your way of thinking I'm no better than a peddler.

"I don't even know my granddaddy's name, much less how much money he had. You can't trace my family tree back to the Civil War and beyond. I was the town drunk's misbehaving kid, so just who the hell do I think I am trying to buy Twenty-two Indigo Place? That's what you're thinking, isn't it?"

She lied. "No."

He shook her slightly. "Well, let me tell you something, Miss Laura Nolan. You're not so high and mighty anymore. I know all about your financial troubles. Your blue blood isn't paying the bills, is it? Your family name isn't putting bread on the table, is it? When you came up empty, the bank didn't give a flip who your granddaddy was. You're busted. So where has all that heritage got you, huh?"

Tears of mortification smarted in her eyes. She couldn't bear his knowing that she was penniless and in debt. "How despicable of you even to mention that." She wrested her arm free. "I don't need you or your money."

"Like hell you don't," he said with a growl. "You're in hock up to your nose, which has always been turned up to me. Whether you like it or not, I'm gonna save your ass. I don't see any other customers in line, clamoring to take Indigo Place off your aristocratic hands. You don't have a choice but to sell it to trash like me, and that's what galls you."

"Take me home," she grated out through her teeth.

"What's got you bugged the most, hmm? That I've got money now and you don't? That James Paden is the one calling the shots? That I'm going to be living in a house I wasn't good enough to darken the door of several years ago?" He paused for emphasis. "Or that I kissed you today and you loved it?"

Seething, she glared up at him. "You can have the house, damn you. Just take me back to my car. Now."

He moved suddenly to take her face between his hands. He yanked her head around to face him when she tried to turn away. "That wasn't the first time, you know," he said softly.

She squeezed her eyes shut. "Please take me back to town."

He stared at her for a long time, his face dark and tense. At last he released her and sat back in his seat. The motor roared to life when he turned the key in the ignition. They said nothing.

The market was closed when they reached it. As soon as he applied the brakes, Laura opened her door and got out. "I'll call Mrs. Hightower tonight." She swiftly shut the door behind her. He didn't drive off until she was safely away from the parking lot.

The shadows the full moon cast into her room were mournful. She lay in bed, thinking how few were the nights she would sleep in this room. The pain was too much to bear. Her heart was broken, and she doubted it would ever be healed. Severing herself from Indigo Place was tantamount to cutting out her heart. How could she live without it?

But that was exactly what she would have to do, because in two days' time it would legally belong to someone else. James Paden's name would be on the deed.

Mrs. Hightower had been predictably giddy when Laura called to tell her that she would accept Mr. Paden's last offer. She didn't mention the hardship he had put her through before she capitulated. The realtor's only concern was that the sale was imminent and that she would get a generous commission from it.

"I have the contract ready. If I get your and Mr. Paden's signatures tonight, we can close the day after tomorrow. Of course, the amount of paper work I'll have to do tomorrow is horrendous, but he was specific about closing as soon as possible."

"The day after tomorrow," Laura cried in alarm. "But that doesn't give me time to pack."

"You'll have time. The contract specifies that you have thirty days to vacate."

That was some consolation, but not much. In thirty days she would have to leave 22 Indigo Place forever. She couldn't bear to think of it. Any more than she could bear to think about the kiss James Paden had given her that morning.

Or the kiss he had later referred to.

For years after it happened, Laura had tried to eradicate that particular memory of him from her mind. Now James had brought it into the forefront, and she must deal with it. Perhaps as an adult she would see the incident from a different perspective. But the familiar ambiguity stole over her as she recalled that night after the football game.

She was in her junior year of high school. It had been a cold Friday night. November. Her breath had frosted in the air as she skipped down the concrete steps of the band building on her way to the waiting school bus.

Exhaust from several motorcycles had also fogged the cold air as they roared up, seemingly from out of nowhere, and formed a ring around her. She was trapped between them and the brick wall of the building.

"Well, what have we got here?" one biker drawled. "I do believe it's one of them twirly girls. What's that they call you, honey?"

"A majorette, stupid," one of his cronies replied. "And she's that, all right. Looks as nimble as a ballerina, don't she?"

They all thought that was immensely funny, and

guffawed loudly. But not loudly enough to attract the attention of the other band members as they climbed aboard the school bus across the parking lot. They were on their way to a postgame party. Because of the football team's victory, everyone was in a celebratory mood. The school bus rocked with laughter and cheering. Someone had taken a drum aboard and a marching cadence was being pounded out. Laura was trapped in the dark shadow of the band building and doubted she could be seen. No one would be coming out behind her, because she had been the last one to leave.

"Let me by," she said in her most condescending tone. Her heart was beating as wildly and loudly as the drum. She recognized the motorcyclists as members of a gang who aimlessly roamed the streets of town looking for mischief. Individually they might not be so bad, but together, goading one another on, they could be dangerous. Laura was sensible enough to be afraid.

One, the first to speak to her, rolled his bike even closer. "Not before you perform for us, twirly girl. We didn't see near enough of you at the football game. Did we, guys?"

His buddies laughed at his cleverness and heartily agreed with him. Encouraged, he reached out and jerked off her letter jacket, leaving Laura standing in the brief, glittery costume she and the other majorettes wore. From the football field, the sparkles showed up well. Up close, they looked flashy and cheap. Laura saw the leering gazes of the men surrounding her, and terror clutched her throat.

She spun away with the intention of running. But she was brought up short by bumping into another cycle she hadn't seen until now. Sitting astride it, a cigarette dangling from his sullen lips, was James Paden, the recognized leader of the gang. Laura hadn't seen much of him since, to the surprise of everyone, he had graduated three years before.

She knew he was working at a garage on the outskirts of town, but she never had occasion to go near a place like that. Any automotive repairs that were needed on her family's cars were handled by Bo. She had seen the Paden boy in town, but the occasions had been few and far between. She had only spoken to him if he spoke to her first.

Once, in the Safeway store, when a vending machine had taken her coins but failed to deliver her Coke, he had come up behind her, banged the machine hard with his fist, opened the forthcoming canned drink, and passed it to her. She had thanked him. He had given her that I-know-what-you-look-like-naked smile and moved on without exchanging a word.

Now she was meeting him face-to-face and they were on his turf. His brows were pulled down low over heavy-lidded, brooding eyes. His jaw was bracketed by the flipped-up collar of his black leather jacket. His thighs were wide-spread as he straddled the idling cycle. He seemed to purr, just as the cycle did, like a cat that had just trapped its dinner.

He drew deeply on the cigarette and blew the smoke into the air until it ghostily wreathed his head. Then he tossed the cigarette onto the asphalt. "Where're you off to in such a hurry, Miss Laura?"

"To—to the band party." She wet her lips nervously, aware of the other five bikers closing in behind her, blocking off any avenue of escape. One made a lewd comment about her legs.

James hitched his chin toward his friends. "The boys and I, we can give you a party."

They snickered. "We sure as hell can," one of them said.

Laura shivered with cold and fear. "I'm supposed to stay with the group."

"D'you always do what you're supposed to?" Paden asked her.

She didn't have time to answer before their attention was drawn toward the bus. It wheezed into motion and rumbled from the deserted parking lot. Horrified, Laura watched its taillights diminish until it was out of sight.

"Now, ain't that a damn shame?" one of the boys behind her said. "They've gone off and left you, twirly girl."

Panicked, Laura looked at James. "Please." Tears filled her eyes.

"Let's see some high-stepping, girl." The speaker swatted her on the bottom.

She whirled around. "Stop it! Don't you dare touch me again."

He frowned. "Now, I'm not sure I cotton to your hoity-toity attitude, sweet thing. What are you bein' so snooty about?"

"She's upset 'cause she forgot her baton. Reckon I'll have to give her another long stick to twirl."

They all burst into raucous laughter at that. The last speaker stepped off his bike. "Let's see how good you are at making new friends." He lunged forward and grabbed her shoulders.

"No!"

Laura screamed and started fighting her attacker. She managed to smack him on the jaw with her doubled fist. Incensed, he cursed, and doubled his efforts to subdue her. His friends came to his aid when Laura proved to be more resistant than they'd bargained on. She fought frantically, though she cried pitiably for help.

"Let her go."

The softly spoken words sliced through the darkness like a rapier. All but one of the cyclists fell back. He was intently mashing his mouth against Laura's while his hand cruelly squeezed her buttock.

"I said to let her go." The words were more incisive this time. The would-be lover raised his head and glanced over his shoulder at his leader.

"Why?"

"Because I said to."

"Aw, hell, she's just carrying on for show. She wants it."

"I'm not going to say it again."

The biker gave some thought to arguing, but his better judgment won out. He knew how dirty Paden could fight, and he didn't want to be on the receiving end of any of it.

As soon as his arms fell to his sides, James reached for Laura's wrist, encircled it, and yanked her forward so hard, her neck almost snapped. "Climb on," he said tersely, indicating the back of the motorcycle seat.

She wasted no time scrambling on behind him. The cold leather was a shock to her bare inner thighs, and she sucked in her breath. The cold air felt good in her mouth, purging it of the beery taste of the kiss she had been subjected to.

"Hand her her coat," James ordered. One of his friends complied. James gave her time to slip her arms into the sleeves before saying, "Later," to his group of faithful followers. Then he gunned the motor of the cycle and it went tearing out of the parking lot and down the street. How they kept from turning over when they took the corner, Laura didn't know.

She didn't know much of anything except a fear that she wouldn't be able to stay on. James must have had the same apprehension, because he turned his head and shouted, "Put your arms around me." Hesitantly, but out of necessity, she slipped her arms around his waist. Beneath the leather jacket, his body was warm. And masculine. Frighteningly so. She'd never touched a boy with this much familiarity. Only, this wasn't a boy. This was a man.

"Where's the party?"

"I don't want to go," she shouted back. "Just take me home, please."

He didn't ask for directions. He knew that she belonged to 22 Indigo Place.

Fast as he drove, he couldn't outrun her fear. The enormity of what she had just escaped caught up with her, and she started crying. Tears streamed down her cheeks, all but freezing on her skin in the frigid wind that blew against her.

For protection, she buried her face against James Paden's neck. He smelled like Old Spice and leather. His hair whipped against her face. When they left the town's streets and the country roads became bumpy, she clung to him more tightly, unconsciously pressing his hips between her thighs.

She knew when he turned onto Indigo Place, but she didn't raise her head until he pulled into the curving driveway of number twenty-two. The house was dark. Her parents had gone out with friends after the football game, thinking that she would be safe at the band party.

The bike came to a full stop, but she didn't move right away. She remained there, clinging to the roughest kid ever to grace the streets of Gregory. Gradually she relaxed her arms.

"You okay?" James asked her, tilting his head back. She met his eyes, thought what nice eyelashes he had, and nodded. "Sure?" Bracing her hands on his shoulders, she climbed off the cycle.

"Yes. Thank you." Her voice was tremulous. Moonlight picked up the wet streaks on her cheeks. Her eyes still looked tearful. They glistened.

James threw his long leg over the bike and stood up in front of her. He studied her face. The corner of his mouth quirked in a fleeting smile. "Your lipstick is smeared."

He raised his hand to her cheek and smoothed his thumb across her lips, picking up the smudged red lipstick she wore only for football games. He made several passes across her mouth, his eyes tracking every slow movement of his thumb.

He was strangely touched by her vulnerability. He had never felt lips so soft. He looked into her eyes. They were wide, innocent, bewildered, and brimming with luminous tears.

Acting purely on instinct, he lowered his head and kissed her. It was a gentle kiss, tender and compassionate. But it was planted fully on her lips. He rubbed his partially opened mouth against hers.

It was by far the most intimate and evocative kiss Laura had ever had. Titillating sensations speared straight downward and found targets in the cradle of her femininity. Her breasts tingled. She reacted by violently pulling back before she could throw her arms around him. The flurry of desire she experienced terrified her, and she suddenly hated the man who had made her feel so unsafe and unsure.

"Did you only rescue me from your friends so you could have me for yourself?"

James looked surprised at her vindictiveness. He even fell back a step. Then the familiar arrogant smirk curled his lip and he gave her an insulting once-over. "You're too bloodless for me, Miss Laura."

He swung his leg over the seat of the bike, stamped on the ignition, and, when the motor caught, shot out of the driveway, spraying gravel on her white patent leather majorette boots.

Laura hadn't seen him again until last evening when he stepped out of the darkness surrounding the porch of her house. As always, James Paden had brought trouble with him. He was acting as her savior again, but, just like that first time, she didn't welcome his interference.

She was dressed in the same suit she had worn to her father's funeral, which fit her mood exactly. Her back was straight and her head held high as she entered the Georgia Land and Title Company. Only those who knew her exceptionally well would ever have guessed that on the inside she was falling apart.

"Good morning, Laura," James Paden said to her a few minutes later as he entered the private office she had been ushered into.

She smiled at him woodenly. "James."

"I hope this time was convenient for you."

She gnashed her teeth in an effort not to shout back at him that there would never be a convenient time to turn her family estate over to him. Barely trusting herself to speak, she said, "I want to get this over with as expeditiously as possible."

He took the chair next to hers. She was disarmed by how "normal" he looked. Normal in the sense that he was dressed like an ordinary businessman, in a correctly tailored three-piece brown suit, an immaculate ivory shirt, and a tasteful brown striped necktie. His cuff links were gold, as was the collar bar beneath his starched collar. His brown shoes were polished to a high gloss. He looked like a prototypical yuppy whom Madison Avenue couldn't have manufactured better. Laura didn't remember ever having seen him in anything but jeans.

His clothes might have suited an executive, but his face, his expression, were as sullen and rebellious as ever, when she dared to look at him eye to eye.

Mrs. Hightower ended her conversation with the title company officer and, with a false sense of importance, came bustling over to the table where Laura and James sat. "Everything is in order and ready for your signatures."

Laura glanced over the mountain of documents and signed each one with dispatch. Mrs. Hightower then passed them to James and he affixed his signature to the specified dotted lines.

Laura divorced her mind from the proceedings. If she thought about what she was doing, she wouldn't be able to carry it out. She merely thought of this meeting as a ritual, much like dental surgery, that one must get through as painlessly as possible, knowing that the outcome will be beneficial.

Finally the title company officer handed her a cashier's check. While Mrs. Hightower was expansively congratulating James on his new home, Laura glanced down at the check.

"There's been some mistake," she said suddenly. Three pairs of eyes registered surprise. "The check," she said, holding it out, "it's too much."

"I'm sure there's been no mistake," the title-company man said, slipping on his reading glasses.

"Mrs. Hightower's commission and the points the seller is supposed to pay haven't been subtracted," Laura explained. On a property that sold for as much as Indigo Place, that was a considerable amount.

"Oh, Mr. Paden took care of all that," Mrs. Hightower said with a relieved smile. "It was stipulated in the contract."

Laura was struck dumb. She glanced at James, who was guiltily studying the toe of his shoe. "I must have overlooked that clause," she muttered.

She endured their drawn out adjournment. When she was free to leave, she sidled up to James and spoke out of the side of her mouth. "May I have a private word with you?"

He smiled down at her. "Sure, baby. I was just about to ask the same of you."

Because of the prying eyes behind typewriters suddenly fallen still, Laura allowed him to take her elbow and escort her through the offices and outside onto the sidewalk. "How about lunch?" he asked as soon as they cleared the door.

"I don't need your charity," she hissed. She smiled for the sake of any busybodies who might still be watching, but her words came out sounding brittle enough to break.

He leaned against the brick wall of the building. "I hardly think inviting you to lunch qualifies as a charitable act."

"Don't be cute with me." She was livid, and felt telltale color filling her cheeks. She only hoped no one else noticed. "I'm talking about the extra money I got from this sale. Mrs. Hightower's commission was to come out of my profit. I was supposed to pay—"

"I felt that I owed that to you."

"You don't owe me anything."

"I bullied you into selling me the property. I wanted to repay you."

"Don't do me any favors. This was a business deal, nothing more. As you so crassly pointed out the other day, I had no choice but to sell. But I'll be damned before I'll take one extra cent from *you*!"

"It's over and done with, Laura. You've already got the cashier's check. I suggest you read contracts more carefully from now on."

"I suggest you go straight to hell." She turned on the heels of her navy blue pumps and stalked off down the sidewalk.

"Does this mean lunch is off?"

The man was insufferable.

She arrived home fuming. Undressing, she pulled off her clothes and tossed them aside as though they were contaminated. *Lunch!* How dare he be civil?

When she had calmed down somewhat, she telephoned her lawyer to tell him she had the check and that it was ready for deposit. "Well, that will be a start," he said with a notable lack of enthusiasm.

"A *start*? I thought this was the answer to our prayers."

"It will certainly pay off the mortgages your father took out on the estate, but we can't stretch it as far as it needs to go." He read through a list of figures.

"Okay, okay," Laura said dismally when he finally reached the end of it. "I guess the extent of my indebtedness just hadn't sunk in. But the house is my only resource. I don't have anything else."

"You have the furnishings," he reminded her quietly.

"But they're *mine*," she protested. "They're heirlooms."

"Priceless heirlooms, Laura." He let her ponder that for a moment. "Besides, what good are they to you now? Where will you put them?"

He had a point. She had already applied at several private schools throughout the South for a teaching position. She wasn't qualified or skilled in anything else, and she liked the idea of hibernating in the sanctuary an exclusive girls' school would provide. But such a job wouldn't pay for a house large or fine enough to accommodate all the furniture that filled the massive rooms of Indigo Place. A storage facility would be an added expense she didn't need.

"I suppose you're right," she conceded. The house was lost to her. Why not the furniture as well? Tears threatened, but she stubbornly held them in check. "How do I go about selling these pieces?"

"Let me handle it."

"I don't want everyone in town to know."

"I understand. I suggest a discreet auction out of town. Atlanta, possibly. Or Savannah, though that might be too close to home."

"Atlanta. Something dignified, please." She had a nightmarish vision of a carnival-barker-type auctioneer braying, "What do I get for this Sheraton sideboard?"

The lawyer assured her he would take care of

everything in a manner agreeable to her. He hung up after reminding her that she only had thirty days to vacate the premises.

That night Laura cried herself to sleep.

When she awoke early, she thought the pounding in her head was a legacy of her weeping and sleeplessness. But she soon realized that the pounding had a distinct ring to it, much like a hammer striking a nail.

Tossing the covers back, she stumbled to the window and threw back the drapes. Her mouth fell open when she saw James Paden wielding a hammer on the gazebo that her father had had built for her twelfth birthday present.

She spun around and raced out of her room and down the stairs. It was so early, the rooms of the house were still dim and cool. She made it to the back porch in record time, hastily unlocked the door, and flung it open.

"Just what the hell do you think you're doing?" she demanded, stepping out onto the flagstone terrace.

The hammer was halted midway between his shoulders and the head of the nail. He glanced over at her and smiled. "Good morning. Did the hammering wake you up?"

"What are you doing?" she repeated.

"Protecting my investment," he answered calmly. He laid the hammer on the ground and came walking toward the terrace, wiping his sweating brow on his sleeve. "It's going to be a hot one today."

"Mr. Paden," she ground out, "I want to know why you're here at this time of day making that infernal racket. I thought I had thirty days to move out." Thirty days of peace. Thirty days without having to see him. She had hoped that she need never see him again.

"You do, but in the meantime I intend to do some repairs around the place. There are several things that need my attention. I don't want the property to get any more run-down than it already is."

She was relieved to know that he hadn't been tearing down the lovely gazebo, but his criticism stung. Sure, the gazebo had needed a few slats replaced, but she hadn't had the money to see that the repairs were done and done properly. She hadn't been neglectful by choice. "You can't do repairs while I'm still here," she said stubbornly.

He braced one foot on the low wall surrounding the terrace and propped his arms on his thigh. Leaning forward, he looked up at her and asked silkily, "Who's going to tell me I can't? I own the place."

She drew a sharp breath, realizing he was right. She was hardly in a position to demand that he leave. And, because it was necessary to inventory the furnishings that were to be auctioned, she couldn't make arrangements to move out before the deadline she'd been granted.

She clamped her lips closed, fiercely disliking her subordinate status and disliking even more the fact that he was aware and taking full advantage of it.

"Then I guess I have no say in the matter, though I think it's inconsiderate of you."

"No one ever accused me of being considerate."

"Kindly let me know when you need to come into the house," she said haughtily. "I don't want you sneaking up on me."

"Why? 'Fraid I'll catch you wearing nothing more than a nightie and a rosy blush?"

She made a high, squeaking sound as she glanced down at herself. He had accurately described her. She had dashed out of her bedroom without remembering to slip on a robe.

Her bare feet virtually flew over the terrace as she beat a hasty retreat through the back door. His low, gruff laughter followed her inside.

Four

If he was going to strut around her house—correction, *his* house—he could at least wear a shirt, Laura thought sourly as she glanced through the kitchen window while she prepared breakfast.

This was the second morning she had awakened to discover James Paden, despoiler of good reputations and carouser extraordinaire, already hard at work on 22 Indigo Place. This morning he was working on the pier that stretched out over the waters of the sound.

Granted, he was attending to things she had had no choice but to overlook, but she resented both his ability to finance the repairs and his ownership of the house, which gave him the right to parade around the place looking any way he liked.

And right now he looked hot and sweaty and damned appealing as he came swaggering across the terrace toward the very door she was surreptitiously peeping through. Laura stepped back out of sight and gave herself a count of ten before she opened the door to his knock.

"Hi."

"Hi." Her response was considerably less cheerful than his. She had taken the time to dress today before she came downstairs, not wanting to be caught in her nightie again. Her jeans were old, her shirt baggy. She had her hair tied up in a scarf.

"Sleep well?" His smile was as pleasant as his tone was polite. Only his eyes gave him away as a maverick. Boldly and without apology, they ranged down her body.

"Yes, fine. Did you need something?"

"A glass of ice water, please. I intended to bring a thermos with me, but forgot it."

None too hospitably she got him the requested drink of ice water. "Thanks. Something sure smells good," he said as he took the glass from her. He quaffed the cold water.

"Bacon. I think it's burning." She rushed to the stove, turned off the burner, and lifted the crisp bacon from the skillet with a pair of tongs.

"I didn't take time to eat this morning," James said wistfully from the doorway. Laura ground her teeth, knowing that he was fishing for an invitation to breakfast. "Guess I'll have to run into town later and pick up a doughnut. 'Course, it'll probably be stale by the time I get there. They start making them about four—"

"Oh, please." She groaned, turning around. "How do you like your eggs?"

He grinned broadly and pulled on the shirt he had kept dangling in his hand. "I thought you'd never ask. And I'll eat eggs any way you want to cook them."

"There's orange juice in the fridge. Help yourself." Her hands were trembling as she cracked additional eggs into the bowl. A piece of shell fell in and she had to pick the elusive, slippery little demon out with the tip of a finger. She mercilessly whipped the eggs to a froth, taking out her agitation on them.

At least he had pulled on his shirt. Earlier, from her hiding place behind the curtain on the kitchen window, she had watched the sun baking his tan even deeper as he bent over the boards he was replacing on the pier. His back was a smooth expanse of supple muscles and bronzed skin.

Glancing at him now, she noticed that he had left most of the buttons on his shirt undone. His chest was more mouth-watering than the tantalizing breakfast smells. It was fantasy-inspiring—hard muscles and lots of soft, curly brown hair a woman's fingers could get lost in.

He had probably worn the old, soft jeans just to aggravate her, Laura thought. They were smeared with grease and paint, threadbare in spots, and indecently snug. His navel was plainly visible above the waistband that rode low on his hips. She didn't even want to think of anything below his waist.

"Do you like them firm?"

Laura dropped her spatula. "What?"

"Scrambled eggs. I don't like them soft."

"Oh, yes, firm. Firm is fine."

Without her having to ask, he passed her two plates and she filled them with the hot, fluffy eggs she had been distractedly stirring around the skillet.

Once everything had been put on the table and coffee poured, they sat down and began eating. "This is good," James mumbled around a bite.

"Thank you. I got in the habit of cooking breakfast for my father every morning before Gladys arrived for work."

"Anybody else?" She looked up inquiringly. "Did you ever cook breakfast for any other man?" He took a sip of coffee.

"My private life is none of your concern, Mr. Paden, as I've mentioned on numerous occasions."

"You cook good. You look good." He assessed her with insolent green eyes. "You'd make some man a good wife."

"Thank you."

"Why didn't you ever get married?"

"Why didn't you?"

"Who said I didn't?"

She glanced up at him quickly. "Are you married?"

"No."

Laura tried not to let her relief show. Why she should care about his marital status she couldn't imagine, other than the idea of kissing a married man appalled her. Of course *he* had kissed *her*, not the other way around. Still, hard as it was to admit even to herself, she liked the idea that he was single.

"But we're not talking about me. We're talking about you," he said. "Tell me why a pretty girl like you never got married."

"I'm a woman," she said starchily. "And I didn't want to get married."

"Hmm. You liked playing the field."

"Something like that," she said dismissively. "More toast?"

"Forgive me, but I just don't see you as the party-girl type."

"Woman," she repeated, stressing the word. "And can we please talk about something besides my love life?"

"Sure," he said, smiling wickedly. "Wanna talk about mine?"

"No!"

He laughed at her emphatic answer. To cover her irritation, she carried their empty dishes to the sink. "If you'll excuse me now, I've got a lot to do."

"Why not take the day off?"

"Take the day off?" He came to stand beside her at the sink, and she looked up at him with incredulity. "I can't. There are a million things I need to do."

"Why don't you come out to the pier and keep me company?" He tucked a strand of hair back into her scarf, then ran his finger down her cheek.

"Sit on that hot pier all day just to watch you work? No, thanks."

"You can sunbathe. And since turnabout's fair play, I'll watch you sunbathe." The tip of his finger batted at her earlobe.

"I don't think so."

"Or you could swim. Then, when I get finished, I could join you in the water. Doesn't that sound like fun?"

It sounded dangerous. Any woman with a grain of sense would do better to wear a suit of armor around him than a swimsuit. "I told you I've got work to do. Are you going to make a pest of yourself for the next thirty days?"

"Twenty-nine."

She shrugged off his hand and turned away, angry over his cruel reminder that in less than a month she would have to leave her home forever.

"Hey, I'm sorry," he said, catching her by the shoulders and turning her around. "I shouldn't have said that. It wasn't kind."

Her shoulders slumped in dejection and the fight

went out of her. "You might just as well speak of it. There's no getting around it."

They stared at each other for a moment. His eyes moved to the top of her head. "Why the scarf? What kind of work are you doing today?"

"I need to inventory the furnishings for auction."

"Auction?" She nodded grimly. "Everything?"

"Almost. I might keep a few of the pieces I cherish most, but I'm going to liquidate as much as I can."

He muttered something under his breath as he turned away. Laura thought she heard him speak her father's name and an obscenity, but she didn't quite catch the conjunction between them.

James left the kitchen. Puzzled, Laura followed him out through the dining room, and found him standing in the entrance hall, gazing into the parlor. His hands were propped on his hips and he was gnawing on his lower lip.

"Say, listen," he said, turning around abruptly, "instead of holding an auction, why not let me buy everything?"

"I . . ." For a moment she was at a loss for words. "You never asked about the furniture."

"I'm asking now. I should've thought of it before. Where would I find furniture better suited to the house than what's already here? Even if I could, it would take a helluva lot of time and trouble. At the end of it, I'd still have second best."

"That's true, only—"

"I'd give you a fair price. We'll itemize the pieces if you want to."

Laura knew from having discussed it with the lawyer that she would make more money selling the furnishings item by item at auction rather than making a blanket sale to one buyer. "All right," she said, spontaneously making up her mind. She'd feel better knowing that Indigo Place was intact even if she weren't residing there any longer.

"Good." Vigorously he rubbed his hands together. "Where do we start?"

"You mean now?"

"Why not? That's what you were going to do today anyway, wasn't it?"

"Yes, but . . ." Compiling a thorough inventory and price list would take hours, days. The idea of spending that much time in the company of James Paden was unnerving. "What about the pier?"

"I can do that anytime."

"There's no reason to trouble yourself with this," she said on a burst of inspiration. "I'll make the list and price the items as I think fair. You can go over the list when I'm finished. If there's any bargaining to be done, we'll do it then."

He hooked his thumbs in his belt loops and gave her a slow, deliberate once-over. "How do I know I can trust you?"

"What!"

"I haven't become rich by buying a pig in a poke."

"A pig—"

"No," he said casually, ignoring her sputtering outrage, "I'll feel much better if we make that list together."

"You're doubting my integrity?" she asked in disbelief. "You were the one caught snitching cookies from the school cafeteria, not me!"

"You remember that?"

"I certainly do."

"I didn't snitch them. The lady in charge of the desserts was slipping them to me. She just wouldn't fess up to it later."

"I don't believe you."

He smiled lazily. "You would if you knew what I was giving her in exchange."

Laura did believe him then. Her cheeks grew hot. To get them back to the subject at hand, she said, "I'm scrupulously honest."

"Then you won't mind if I look over your shoulder while you're making that list."

She drew a deep breath and expelled it on a long gust of annoyance. "I'll get a tablet and *two* pencils." She stamped toward the Queen Anne secretary in the parlor.

"Don't we get a lunch break?"

Laura laid her tablet aside and looked at her "assistant" with asperity. "You had breakfast."

"Yeah, about five hours ago. I'm hungry."

He was looking at her mouth. Uneasily she put space between them. Her own stomach was experiencing pangs, and they weren't caused by hunger of the digestive variety.

They had begun taking inventory in the dining room. After listing the pieces of furniture, they had started going through the china cabinets and silver chests. It was a painstaking, time-consuming project, hampered by James's penchant for joking and idle conversation. He had shown an inordinate amount of interest in the events of her life since he had last seen her, over ten years ago.

"I need something to tide me over," he said plaintively.

"What did you have in mind?" When she glanced up at him, she wished she hadn't asked. According to his expression, a meal was only one of their options.

"For food, you mean?"

"Of course for food."

"A picnic."

"A picnic?"

"You stay here." He pushed himself off the chair he had been straddling with his chin propped on its back. "I'll scrounge around for something and bring it in."

"Do you trust me now?" she asked, batting her eyelashes in farcical innocence.

"About as far as you trust me," he said over his shoulder as he sauntered out. Laura made a face at him, but he didn't see it.

He returned several minutes later carrying a plastic tray loaded with fruit and cheese, an assortment of crackers, and two tall glasses of iced tea. He set the tray down on the floor near the wide windows and dropped down beside it. "Come on over."

"You really meant it when you said a picnic, didn't you?"

"Yep. But better. No ants."

"Mother, Father, and I used to have picnics on Sunday afternoons in the summertime," she said musingly, sitting down beside him and leaning against the windowsill.

He topped a cracker with cheese spread and passed it to her. "The Padens weren't known for their Sunday picnics." His comment was made without rancor. "I guess I'm making up for the ones I missed when I was a kid."

She nibbled on the cracker, sorry that she had unthinkingly mentioned her family. Comparisons of their social statuses were bound to be drawn. Laura acknowledged that she'd been born with the proverbial silver spoon in her mouth.

It was a wonder that James didn't hate her. Or did he? Was that why he wanted 22 Indigo Place? Did he know that selling her family home to him would be the most bitter pill for her to swallow? Because she typified those who had snubbed him, was he punishing her?

"I'm sure your mother is glad you can go on picnics together now." Laura looked at him slyly. His jaw tensed.

"I wouldn't know."

"Haven't you seen her?"

"No."

"At all?"

"No."

"Does she know you're back?"

He shrugged. "She might have gotten wind of it."

Laura was shocked and a trifle disappointed in him because he hadn't contacted his mother. The last time she had seen Mrs. Paden, she was certainly better dressed than she had been years ago, but she still had that weary, dejected, woebegone look that had always characterized her in Laura's mind. How could he neglect his only relative so unconscionably?

Suddenly he reached out and whipped the scarf off Laura's head. Her sun-lightened brown hair tumbled to her shoulders. "That's better."

"Why'd you do that?" she asked irritably.

"Why'd you tie that thing around your hair?" he fired back.

"I wanted—"

"You wanted to make yourself as unattractive as possible."

"That's ridiculous. Why would I do that?"

"So I wouldn't lust after your body." She closed her mouth with a soft click of her teeth. "Right?" He bit into a crunchy slice of apple. Several moments elapsed. She couldn't think of a single thing to say. "Cat got your tongue?"

"I never heard anything so preposterous."

He chuckled low and deep. "I can see straight through you, Miss Laura. Just like I could see through that nightie you had on yesterday morning. Did you hope I'd forget how adorable and tousled you looked fanning around in that?"

"I wish you would forget it."

"Not likely. I'll remember how you look first thing in the morning for a long time." Brazenly he looked at her breasts. "How everything looks."

"I've had enough." She dropped a slice of cheese back onto the tray.

His hand shot out and caught her wrist before she could get to her feet. "I'm not finished yet."

"But I don't want any more."

"Where are you going?"

"Back to work."

"Stay with me."

"I don't want to."

"Scared?"

"*What?*"

"You heard me."

"Of course I'm not scared."

"You used to be. Are you still that frightened little bunny, Laura?"

"I don't know what you're talking about?"

"Is it me you're afraid of? Or is it the male sex in general?"

"I'm not afraid of anybody. Certainly not you."

"Good. Then you'll stay here with me while I finish my lunch," he said blandly, releasing her hand and stretching out on his side. He propped his elbow on the floor and supported his cheek in his palm. He continued to munch on the snacks, but kept his eyes trained on her. They, as much as his steely grip only moments earlier, effectively kept Laura anchored there beside him. She wouldn't lose face by moving away from him now.

On the surface she registered nothing but cool composure and a trace of hauteur, but inwardly she was seething. "Why do you think I'm afraid of you?" she asked, unable to hold back the question.

"It's either that or you're a snob."

"Why do you say that?"

"Because you always ran when you saw me coming."

"You were bad news. As far as I'm concerned you still are."

He laughed out loud at that. "Damn, I like you! I always did."

"You didn't even know me."

"No, but what I knew, I liked. Shy, prissy little Laura Nolan has a mean stinger when she's pushed too far." He laid his free hand on her arm and stroked it with his fingertips. "I always wondered just how far I could go with you."

"You found out that night you brought me home on your motorcycle. When I wouldn't let you kiss me, you said I was bloodless."

His eyes focused on her mouth. "That was then. This is now." He slid his hand beneath her sleeve and stroked the bend of her elbow. "How hot do you get before you burn?"

She yanked her arm away from him and scooted across the floor to get out of touching distance. She hadn't known that the inside of her elbow was so supersensitive. "Speaking of burning," she said inanely, "I saw you race one time on television. Your car spun out of control and caught on fire."

He grinned at her adroit change of subject, but let it pass without comment. "You'll have to be more specific. That happened several times."

"Were you ever hurt?"

"Not extensive injuries."

"Were you ever afraid?"

"Nope." He pushed another cracker into his mouth.

"Never?"

He shook his head. "Anxious, maybe. Excited. Never afraid. There's not much to fear when you don't care if you live or die."

Laura stared at him speechlessly, gauging his sincerity. The eyes that stared back at her were compelling and truthful. He wasn't jesting. He meant it. "And you didn't?"

"Not for several years."

"But now you do?"

"Yes, now I do."

He didn't seem inclined to elaborate, so she didn't press him to. "You were a very good race-car driver, from what I understand. You must have enjoyed it."

"I loved it."

"What's it like?"

"Having sex."

He grinned at her startled expression. Rolling onto his back, he stacked his hands beneath his head and gazed up at the ceiling as he talked.

"All that tremendous power continues to build until it trembles around you. The heat. The thrust of the engine. The driving pistons. The friction. Then there comes that moment, an instant, when you have to give it all you've got. You don't care what's on the other side of the finish line; at that point you'll risk anything to get there. You open full throttle and let it explode. You've got no choice. Just like sexual climax."

When he stopped talking, the silence was palpable. Slowly he turned his head and looked up at Laura. Her eyes were glassy. She was held in thrall by his entrancing words and the raspy whisper in which he had spoken them.

Moving slowly, he laid his hand on her thigh, squeezing lightly. "Understand what I mean?"

"I think so."

He rolled to a sitting position. He was close. The hooded green eyes invited her to jump inside them and drown.

She was tempted. The appeal James Paden had exuded as a youth was nothing compared to the magnetism he now possessed. As a high-school girl, Laura had felt the tug of his allure, but hadn't recognized it for what it was. Now she did. It was lust. The aura of danger that surrounded him, his sullen expression, promised undiscovered delights if a woman were only brave enough to risk the consequences of finding them.

The penalties for such recklessness were high. Laura knew countless girls who had tried for years to live down the bad reputations James Paden had helped them earn. Was she insane? Why was she sitting here talking about sexual climax with such a man?

Forcibly shaking off her trance, she stood up and said, "I guess we should get back to work."

He stood up with her and linked his hard fingers around each of her wrists. "Sure about that? You know what they say about all work and no play." His lips swept her cheek fleetingly. "I'd love to play with you."

Laura pulled her hands free. "I thought you were here to work. If you don't want to, then leave. I'm busy." She turned away, but not before she saw the treacherous grin spread across his moody face. Far from being daunted, he was merely amused.

The project took them three days, three days spent almost entirely and exclusively in each other's company. He arrived with sacks of groceries the morning after their picnic, explaining over Laura's vehement protests that if he was going to take meals with her, he was going to provide some of the food.

Laura didn't like sharing anything with him— time, food, space. But she had no say in the matter, no more so than she did about the way he touched her, which was often.

He contrived reasons to have his hands on her frequently. No one, especially someone as agile as he, was *that* clumsy. Often he would stumble like a bad comic. To break his fall, he would clasp her tightly against him.

And she knew his manners didn't constrain him to assist her down the stairs or through a door or around a piece of furniture, but he was always doing chivalrous things like that, too. What worried her most was that she came to enjoy his manhandling.

During those three days, she grew to like him more than she'd imagined she ever could. He was an entertaining conversationalist and an even better listener. He encouraged her to tell him the stories about 22 Indigo Place that she had heard at her grandmother's knee. Surprisingly, he was genuinely interested in the history of the house. She discovered that he had a keen, if somewhat caustic, sense of humor, and that he wasn't without sensitivity.

While they were taking inventory of the master suite, they came across numerous silver frames preserving pictures of several generations of Nolans. Laura methodically listed the frames in her tablet.

Moments later, James took the tablet from her and marked through this latest addition.

"What are you doing?" she asked when he wordlessly handed the tablet back to her.

"These pictures mean a lot to you, don't they?"

"I can take the pictures out."

"But the frames were made for them. Keep the frames. A present from me," he added quickly when he saw she was about to object.

"Thank you."

"You're welcome."

He picked up one of the frames and studied the photograph. "Who's this?"

"My paternal grandparents. Franklin and Maydell Nolan." She felt very tender toward him as he gazed down at the old photograph. "James, you told me the other day that you didn't even know your grandfather's name. Is that true?"

He set that frame down and picked up another. "Not on my old man's side, no. He was a bastard . . . in more ways than the most literal. Paden was my grandmother's maiden name. She died when he was just a kid, during the depression sometime. That's all I know about it."

She couldn't come up with an expression of sympathy that didn't sound banal, so she chose to remain silent. He exchanged frames again and smiled down at the photograph. "Is this you?"

She leaned over his arm to study the picture. "That's me. Skinny and toothless. My grandpa had just hung a swing in the big live oak for me."

"The one that's still there?"

"Yes. Mother went running back to the house to get the camera. I'm glad she had the foresight to take our picture together. I think that's the only . . . What's the matter?" she asked suddenly when she chanced to glance up at him. He was studying her intently.

"I was just thinking what a cute little kid you were."

"I look terrible! Look at those pigtails." She laughed, pointing down at the picture. "My knees were so knobby and continually scabbed over."

He studied the picture again and laughed. "Come to think of it, you were kinda scrawny. Guess I just favor little girls no matter how they look."

"And big girls."

Her breasts were shelved on his hard forearm. He looked down at them before meeting her gaze. "Yeah. I like big girls too."

Laura backed away from him, her face suffused with color. "When we finish in here, we'll be through."

They worked for another hour before the tedious task was finally completed. Laura led him downstairs. "If it's all right with you," he said, "I'm going to take another look at the pier before I leave for the day. I want to see how much more lumber I'm going to need."

"All right. While you're doing that, I'll run these figures through the adding machine." She indicated the tablet, with its lengthy list. "I want to get this settled as soon as possible."

"Give me a bill this afternoon and I'll bring you a check in the morning."

Laura went into her father's study and ran the price list through the adding machine several times, until the final sum was verified. It was impressive, and the money would go a long way to pay off her debts. She hoped there'd even be some left over—if James didn't haggle her down too much.

When he returned from his inspection of the pier, she nervously presented him with the total.

She had stepped out onto the porch to meet him when she saw him coming across the yard. Now she braced herself for a wrangling match. It never came. He hardly glanced down at the tape she had so painstakingly checked and double-checked.

"Fine. Whatever." He folded the tape and stuck it in the breast pocket of his shirt.

She felt as if she'd been denied her day in court. "Fine? Whatever? Is that all you have to say?"

"Yes."

She pointed toward his pocket. "But you didn't even check the list!"

"I trust you. I was just kidding when I said I didn't." He chucked her under the chin. "I'll buy everything for the full amount, but I want you to feel free to take anything you want as a personal memento."

"Wait a minute," she cried when he turned his back and started down the wide front steps. "If you were going to buy everything, why did we just spend days itemizing every single object under the roof? Why did you have me make that damn price list in the first place?"

He propped his shoulder against a column and folded his arms across his chest. "You sure you really want to know?"

No, she was positively sure she didn't. Not while he was wearing that lecherous smile and his eyes were sultry with suggestion. "It was an utter waste of time," she muttered crossly.

"I take exception to that, Miss Laura. Now I know where everything is, down to the Christmas decorations. I know all the stories behind the house, where ordinarily I wouldn't. And"—he stressed the word—"I've had a good time."

"Well, I haven't. I could have been doing—"

"What?"

She frantically searched her mind for something she could have been doing. "Well, *something*. As a seller I think I've gone farther than the extra mile, so if you'll excuse me now, I'll say good-bye." She stormed toward the front door.

"I don't guess this is a good time to be asking favors, is it?"

She came to a dead stop. Assuming her most autocratic expression, she stiffly pivoted to face him again. "What?" she asked coldly.

"Would you mind if I brought my girl out to see the house?"

Several seconds ticked by while Laura mutely stared at him. If the floorboards of the porch had just been jerked out from under her, she didn't think she would have fallen any farther. She hit bottom hard. It was jarring. "Your girl?"

He pushed himself away from the column and smiled. "Yeah, my girl. I call her Tricks." He winked. "She's been dying to see the place ever since I bought it. And I think she ought to give it a look-see before we move in."

Over my dead body, Laura wanted to say.

"Would tomorrow be convenient?"

She bit her tongue to keep from telling him to go straight to hell and to take Tricks with him. But he was the owner of the house. And he hadn't quibbled over the price of the furnishings. He had the right to bring anybody he wanted to to see the house. What could she say to stop him? His appalling bad taste wasn't reason enough for her to refuse him permission. She doubted it would do any good to say no anyway.

But the insensitivity of his request had a profound effect on her. The affront affected her physically, viscerally. More than making her angry, she couldn't move or speak. She was afraid she was going to be ill all over the front porch.

That jealousy was the source of her sudden attack of nausea was unthinkable, yet the emotion that churned through her felt very much like jealousy.

"What time?" She forced her mouth to form the words.

"Around midmorning. She likes to sleep late."

Laura nodded. "That will be fine."

Five

Fool, fool! Laura cursed herself the next morning as she dressed. Why had she been so obliging? Why, when he had asked his "favor," hadn't she told him what a lowlife she thought he was? During her sleepless night, she had called him every disparaging name she could think of. Why hadn't she called him those names to his face? She wished she had demonstrated the full extent of her contempt when he had provided her with such a prize opportunity.

Tricks! "I'll just bet," Laura muttered as she pulled a cotton knit sleeveless sweater over her head.

She envisioned Tricks as the stereotypical indulged mistress of a wealthy man, complete with a marabou-trimmed negligee and a mountain of lace-edged pillows on which she reclined. She slept until noon, only arising in time to watch soap operas through eyes puffy from dissipation while she poked chocolates into her petulant mouth.

Laura brushed her hair with a vengeance, thinking that Tricks would no doubt be a brassy bottled blond. She applied the lightest, most subtle floral perfume she had, thinking that in a short while 22 Indigo Place would probably be reeking of musk.

The new lady of the manor was named Tricks!

It didn't bear thinking about. Her ancestors must be spinning in their graves. Had her father known the repercussions of his carelessness, he surely would have been a more conscientious money manager. Would anyone ever have imagined that the Nolan family estate would fall so low as this?

What galled Laura most was that she had actually started liking James Paden. "Ha!" she shouted to the walls as she descended the staircase in a militant march. "You can't make a silk ear . . . a silk purse . . . oh, whatever," she finished in exasperation when she couldn't remember how the adage went. All she knew was that it fit.

She had even felt a twinge of pity for him yesterday when they were looking at the pictures of her grandparents. He had looked so vulnerable, his hair falling over his brow in the way that used to make the girls at Gregory High School swoon. His lower lip had looked even fuller than usual, his eyes more brooding. There had even been a moment there when she'd been tempted to brush back his hair, offer him comfort, offer him . . .

"Never mind," she mumbled. But her brain wasn't listening. In her mind there was a vivid picture of them lying entwined on the carpeted floor of the master suite. She was rendering him the tenderness he needed, and he was rendering her the passion so absent from her life.

Far too often she thought about his kiss. It had been insulting. She'd dated men, some over a period of months, but none had ever dared to kiss her in such an evocative way. It had been the most sexual kiss she'd ever experienced, and she wished she could forget it.

However, she had the disturbing impression that she would remember it for as long as she lived. Just as she remembered the night he had brought her home on his motorcycle so many years ago. There was something about James Paden's touch that a woman couldn't wash off. It remained on her forever, as indelible an imprint as a tattoo.

But as memorable as the kiss had been for her, it had been routine and meaningless to him. He had probably already forgotten it, Laura thought bitterly. She wondered if he had kissed her only because Tricks had been unavailable that night.

Before she had time to ruminate more, she heard the distinctive growl of the sports car's motor. She stood behind the parlor drapes, where she would have a full view of James and Tricks while staying out of sight.

The car rolled to a stop. Its windows were tinted, so Laura couldn't see inside. James was the first one out. He went around the rear of the car, looking pridefully up at the house.

"Show-off," Laura mouthed from her hiding place. And didn't he *ever* look bad? This morning's jeans were in slightly better condition than those he'd been wearing all week to work in. They were starched, and creased down the front of his trim legs. He had on a polo shirt, but the collar was flipped up, dispelling any notion that he had gone preppy.

He bent down and opened the passenger car door, extending his hand inside. Laura caught her lower lip between her teeth and pinched her eyes closed for a moment before opening them again.

When she did, she went perfectly still and stared

blankly at the couple walking hand in hand up the steps. Out of sheer spite, she had planned to let them wait for an interminable amount of time on the porch before she answered the doorbell. But as soon as the chime pealed through the house, she hurried to the front door and pulled it open.

"Good morning, Laura."

"Good morning," she answered huskily, not quite sure her voice would work at all.

"I'd like you to meet Tricks," James said, pushing his companion forward. "My daughter."

Laura and James stared at each other for a lengthy moment before she looked down at the little girl standing between them.

"Hello, Miss Nolan." She spoke the words carefully and clearly, as though they had been rehearsed.

Laura's heart melted and there was a tightening in her throat. She knelt down in front of the child. "Hello. And please call me Laura."

"My real name's Mandy. 'Cept my daddy calls me Tricks." She tilted her head back to smile up at him.

"Tell her why," he suggested, returning her smile.

Laura noticed that she had wide green eyes, spattered with gold flecks. "He did magic tricks for me. I liked them so much he started calling me that. But that was when I was little and now I'm big."

"She got too clever for me," James said, laughing. "She could spot even my most subtle sleight-of-hand movements."

"Do you like magic tricks?" Mandy asked Laura seriously.

"Very much."

"Maybe my daddy will do some for you sometime. He's real good at it."

Laura glanced up at the object of Mandy's admiration. He was smiling down at his daughter with unabashed love and adoration. "I'm sure he is." Laura stood up. "I was just about to have some coffee cake. Would anyone else care for some?"

"I would," Mandy piped up eagerly. Then she winced and glanced up at her father. "Is it okay, Daddy?"

"As long as Laura invited you to, it's okay."

"Come on, Mandy, I'll show you into the kitchen."

Laura offered the little girl her hand and Mandy took it without a second's hesitation. She appeared to be a well-adjusted child, harboring no bashfulness toward a stranger. Her long hair, the same saddle-brown color as James's, had been neatly brushed and secured on the sides with barrettes. Her sundress was spotlessly clean, the ruffles ironed. She was wearing a pair of sandals on her plump little feet.

"This sure is a big house," she said with awe as they passed through the dining room.

"You'll know your way around in no time," Laura assured her with a smile. "See, here's the kitchen already."

They stepped into the sunny room, and Laura offered Mandy a chair at the table. She hadn't planned on serving the Tricks of the marabou and pillows anything but a surly disposition, but thanks to Sara Lee, she produced the promised coffee cake and sliced Mandy a generous portion. She placed a tall glass of milk beside the plate and furnished her with a napkin and fork. James declined the cake, but Laura poured them coffee and they joined his daughter at the table.

Mandy ate with the universal childish appreciation of anything sweet, but had good table manners. When a chunk of cake fell off her fork into her lap, she looked up at James contritely. "That's all right, Tricks," he said softly. "It was an accident. Just slip it back onto your plate."

"How old are you, Mandy?" Laura asked to smooth over the rough spot.

"Five and a half. Do you have a Cabbage Patch doll?"

"Uh, no," Laura said, laughing slightly. "Do you?"

"Uh-huh."

"Say, 'Yes, ma'am.' "

She covered her mouth with a chubby hand. "I forgot."

James winked at her, letting her know he was reminding, not scolding, her. She beamed a smile at him and turned back to Laura. "My doll's name is Annmarie. I brought her with me, but Daddy said she had to wait in the car. Do you think she can see our new room later?"

"Of course."

"I think you're pretty."

"Thank you, Mandy. I think you are too."

"Daddy said you were pretty, but I was afraid you'd be old, or something."

Laura wouldn't have looked at James then to save her life. "If you're finished with your cake, why don't you let me show you through the house?"

The child was eager to explore, though she seemed intimidated at first by the immensity of the rooms. By the time they reached the second story, however, she had overcome her timidity and her eyes were shining.

"Is this going to be my room?" she squealed, racing into Laura's bedroom. Ruffled skirt bouncing, she dashed to the windows, then to the cheval glass in the corner, then to the dresser, then to the bed. "It looks like a princess's room. Is this where I'll sleep, Daddy?"

"We'll see," he said, noticing the sad expression on Laura's face. "Right now I want to show you around outside."

"Let me see if I know my way to the front door," Mandy said, running between James and Laura.

"Enjoy your tour. I'll see you later," Laura said quietly as James followed his daughter out of the bedroom.

"Aren't you coming?" Laura shook her head.

Mandy, overhearing, paused at the top of the stairs. "Oh, please, Laura. *Please.* Daddy said you know everything about In—Indi—about this house."

James's compelling eyes seconded his daughter's plea. One pair of those green eyes Laura might have resisted, but not two. "All right."

The three of them trooped outside. Mandy beat a path to the shore of the sound, but waited obediently, if impatiently, when James called for her not to go farther without him. After they walked the length of the pier and back, they toured the empty stables—the horses had been the first to go when Laura realized the financial situation she was in.

"Can I have a pony, Daddy?"

"They require a lot of attention. Would you take care of one?"

Mandy nodded solemnly. "I promise."

"Then I'll keep my eye out for a pony that needs a home."

Shrieking in delight, Mandy made a mad dash for the swing that hung from the massive branches of the live oak tree. James pushed her in it. Her giggles were infectious. By the time he was worn out, Laura was leaning against the trunk of the tree, smiling.

"Congratulations on her, James. She's wonderful."

"She is, isn't she?" He felt it was his right to be boastful. For a moment Laura and he watched Mandy as she addressed a snail making his slow progress across the ground.

"I wish you had told me about her," Laura remarked in mild reproach. "I would have been spared the shock."

His attention switched from his child to the woman standing beside him. She was self-consciously plucking leaves off the lowest branches of the tree. "It shocked you to find out I had a daughter?"

"Frankly, yes."

He leaned forward and whispered seductively, "Do you doubt my potency?"

She blushed and tried to laugh off his question. "Of course not."

"I'll be glad to demonstrate it."

"James!" she admonished. "It's just that you don't quite fit my image of a doting parent."

He looked chagrined. "That's reasonable. In my rebellious youth I swore I'd never be shackled."

"Obviously you aren't."

"Aren't what? Shackled?"

"You said you weren't married."

"I'm not."

"Oh."

He was amused by her discretion. "If you want to know about Mandy's mother, why don't you come right out and ask?"

"What about Mandy's mother?"

Her blunt question surprised him, and he laughed. But his face became serious when he began to speak. "I didn't mention either of them because I didn't want you to have any preconceived notions."

Mandy was obviously illegitimate, but Laura would never cruelly label a child, and she took umbrage at his thinking she would. "I'm not as narrow-minded as that." All she was guilty of was consumptive curiosity over the woman who had borne James Paden a child whether she was married to him or not. "Is she with you?"

"Who? Mandy's mother? God forbid."

"You mean . . ." Laura was at a loss. "I don't understand."

He braced his shoulder against the trunk of the tree and gazed down at her. "Look, Laura, she was a tramp, okay? A groupie who followed race-car drivers around the circuit. She hung out in the bars we all patronized at night. She was available and on the make. Usually I'm more discriminating than that, but one night I got careless, a little drunk, and she ended up in my bed."

Laura, unable to maintain eye contact, lowered hers to his throat. He really had lived beyond the pale. He had moved in circles she couldn't even fathom. His lifestyle was as like hers as an Eskimo's to a Bedouin's. How many women *had* ended up in his bed, carelessly or otherwise? And foolishly she had read so much into a single kiss!

"Anyway," he said, recapturing her attention, "she managed to latch on and I was too indifferent to send her away. When she told me she was pregnant, I reacted typically. I was furious. Primarily I wanted to know if the kid was mine. When she swore to me it was, I accepted the responsibility for it. But all she demanded of me was money for an abortion."

He looked at Mandy, his eyes distant. "Then,

hell, I don't know what happened to me." He sighed and ran his fingers through his hair. "I got to thinking, you know? That was *my kid*. And we were planning to kill it before it even had a chance to live. God knows life can be rough, but everybody should be granted the chance to give it a shot."

He didn't wait for Laura to respond. He was still rationalizing that uncharacteristic decision he had made to keep his child.

"So I told Mandy's mother I wanted her to have the baby. The bitch carried on for weeks, saying she didn't want to be pregnant. Finally she reconciled herself to my stubbornness. To shut her up, I promised her a hefty amount of money and her freedom once the baby was born. I even browbeat her into marrying me so the baby would be legitimate."

He glanced down at the crown of Laura's head. She stood still with head bowed, listening. "Those nine months were the longest I've ever spent in my life. There were plenty of times when I regretted my decision. I wanted that bitch out of my life. But then I'd start thinking about the baby and that would give me the stamina to tolerate its mother for another day. Then another, until Mandy was born."

An uncontainable smile broke across his face when he turned his head to look at his daughter again. "She was worth it. Lord, she was beautiful."

"What happened to her mother?" Laura asked hoarsely, incredibly moved by the story.

He shrugged. "As soon as she was able, she split and got a quickie, uncontested divorce, giving me sole custody of Mandy. I saw her several times after that, hanging out around the race tracks. But that was several years ago. She wants nothing to do with us. And that's fine with me."

"But Mandy's her child!" Laura couldn't believe the woman's disregard for her own baby.

"Someone with your values can't understand that kind of desertion, but she was worthless. I wasn't exaggerating when I said she was a tramp."

"Once you got successful in business—"

"Oh, she tried to get money from me. Once. I nipped that in the bud."

The fierceness of his expression indicated to Laura that she was better off not asking exactly how he had "nipped" it. "Was it difficult for you to handle the baby alone?"

"By the time Mandy came along, I could afford to hire a nanny. But the transient lifestyle was no good. That's why I gave up racing. Besides, it was too dangerous."

Laura gazed up at him with dawning realization. "That's when you started caring whether you lived or died."

"Yes," he said softly. "That's when I started feeling fear. I didn't want to make Mandy an orphan. So I went into business. The rest you know."

"You never considered giving her up for adoption? I mean, I can understand your wanting to give her life. But you took on a tremendous responsibility."

He laughed in self-derision. "I know it sounds crazy, but I wanted my baby very much, regardless of who her mother was."

"Why, James?"

"I think," he began slowly, "it was because when I was a kid, I never had anything brand-new. Anything I ever owned was secondhand. It had belonged to someone else before it was passed down to me." His fingers closed into a fist. "She was mine. She belonged to me. And she would love me."

He drew himself up, defensive because he had revealed too much of himself. "I guess someone like you would find that hard to understand."

Laura was seeing a side of James Paden that few, if any, knew about. He wasn't nearly as hard and tough as he wanted everyone to believe. It was just that life had dealt him a rotten hand, and he had played it by bluffing. His toughness was a defense mechanism. He was as vulnerable as the next person, certainly where his daughter was concerned.

"I understand." She didn't have an opportunity to expound, because Mandy ran up at that moment and took each of their hands in hers. "Show me that little white house with the holes in it." She pointed at the gazebo. "Please, Laura, Daddy."

They spent another hour traipsing around the estate, mostly in pursuit of Mandy, whose energy was boundless. By the time they reentered the house, Laura was wilted. "How do you keep up with her?" She laid her hand against her heaving chest. They had completed their tour by having a foot race back to the house. She had placed third.

"It's not easy," James conceded with a laugh as he wiped his brow with his sleeve. "I'm sorry for the imposition."

"I don't feel imposed upon. I enjoyed it."

He took a step closer and stared down into her dewy face. "Did you?"

Their voices had become hushed in the shadowed entrance hall. "Yes."

"Laura—"

"Laura, this is Annmarie," Mandy said, bounding through the front door. She had retrieved the doll from the car and was holding it up proudly.

Laura dragged her eyes away from James's smoky stare and knelt down for a formal introduction to Annmarie. When she straightened, the previous mood had vanished and couldn't be recaptured. She was both greatly relieved and vaguely disappointed. What had he been about to say before Mandy's interruption?

"We're going out for a late lunch, Laura. Care to join us?" he asked.

"Oh, say yes," Mandy urged, tugging on Laura's skirt and hopping up and down. "Say yes, please."

"I'm sorry, I can't." Laura smoothed her hand over Mandy's glossy hair. "I have an appointment in town." James had unceremoniously slipped her a check for the furnishings. Now that she had it, she was going to deposit it in the bank immediately and notify her lawyer that he could start paying off her bills.

No amount of wheedling or arguing from either James or Mandy could change her mind. Finally they gave up and said their good-byes. Laura bent down and smiled at Mandy. "I hope you enjoy living in Indigo Place as much as I did when I was a little girl."

"Did you sleep in my room?"

"Yes. Will you and Annmarie always take care of it for me?" Mandy's usually animated face was serious as she nodded. "Good. Thank you." On the brink of tears, Laura straightened.

James said, "I'm coming back in the morning to do some chores. I'll see you then."

Not trusting herself to speak, she merely bobbed her head in acknowledgment. She waved to Mandy, whose exuberance had been restored, as they drove away.

Laura's errands didn't take up nearly as much time as she had hoped they would. She returned to number twenty-two just as the sun was setting. Dusk had always been a sad time for her anyway.

When she entered the house, the rooms were rosy with twilight. An unbearable sadness settled over her.

She went upstairs and turned on the lamp in her bedroom. The long shadows it cast against the walls emphasized the pervading loneliness. The small sounds she made as she peeled off her clothing hardly relieved the gloomy silence.

Twenty-two Indigo Place needed people in it. A family. James and Mandy were a family. The child's laughter had made the stately rooms ring with new life. Laura was being selfish to stay when the Padens needed a home.

What justification did she have for staying the full time allotted? Now that the furniture had been sold, there was really no need to delay her departure. She had received several responses to her applications for teaching jobs. It would take her only a few days to pack what few belongings she had left, load up her car, and leave. She could travel on a frugal budget to her interviews until she got a job and found a new place to live.

Beyond the practical considerations were the emotional ones.

She missed James when he wasn't around. His sullen face and sultry eyes had come to be so familiar, she saw them in her dreams. His voice, laced with insolence and innuendo, was no longer aggravating, but endearing. The way he moved and the way he smelled and the way he dressed were now the standards by which she judged other men.

Her life hadn't been the same since he roared up out of the darkness on his motorcycle. He made her think. He made her laugh. He made her tingle.

How stupid could she be? What a ridiculous, pathetic woman she was. To fall in love with a man like him was calamitous. Yet that was exactly what had happened. Like so many before her, she had fallen victim to his charm, which amounted to no charm at all. That was what made him so irresistible. His I-don't-give-a-damn-about-anything attitude was a challenge to every female he met. Each one fancied herself the single woman who could shake his unshakable insouciance.

But prim and proper Miss Laura Nolan couldn't begin to entice James Paden, so harboring the fantasy that she might pique his interest, much less his lust, was absurd. She must leave before she did something really stupid and made a complete fool of herself.

She would tell him tomorrow. It would hurt, but it would only hurt more later on, because she was coming to love him more every day.

Tomorrow.

By the time she came downstairs for coffee, his car was already in the driveway. She glanced through the windows of several rooms, but didn't spot him anywhere outside. After drinking several cups of coffee to fortify herself for the encounter that must take place, she ventured outdoors. She hadn't noticed it before, but the sky was overcast. Low clouds threatened rain, and Laura shivered against the stiff breeze.

The pier was the first place she looked for James, though she didn't see him anywhere around. She was making her way back toward the house when it began to rain. It wasn't a light shower that gradually built into a downpour; it started out as a torrent. One moment she was dry, and the next she was being pelted with heavy rain. She ran for the first available shelter, the stable.

It was dark inside the cavernous building. It

smelled like hay and horses and leather, not at all unpleasant to someone who had grown up enjoying horseback riding.

Laura shook the raindrops from her hair. Standing just inside the door she looked out at the silver curtain of rain that fell between her and the house.

"Gotcha!"

She let out a sharp yelp of fright and surprise as her arms were clasped from behind. She was turned around and brought face-to-face with James. "Scare you?"

"You know you did!" she said, faking exasperation. Actually her heart began racing at the sight of him. "I didn't know you were in here."

"Aw, shucks. I thought that was why you came tearing in here."

"I only came tearing in here to get out of the rain."

He glanced over her shoulder. "It's really coming down." Then he looked her straight in the eye. "We might be in here for a long time."

Laura was certain the serpent had said something to that effect to Eve.

James hadn't released her. His hands were warmly curled around her upper arms. Her breasts were flattened against his chest. He gazed down at her. She wet her lips nervously.

"What were you doing in here?"

"Hmm?" he asked absently. His eyes were taking in the raindrops that covered her hair like a glistening net. "Oh, I was, uh . . ."

He took several steps forward, propelling her backward. "James?"

"Hmm?" He continued to study her face.

"You were about to say something," she whispered on a thin breath when her back came up against the wall.

"I was?"

"Yes."

With his hands on her shoulders, he pinned her against the wall, lowered his head, and settled his mouth firmly against hers. Angling his head, he sealed their mouths together. Any protests that might have been forthcoming were trapped inside Laura's mouth. Her lips responded to the warm pressure of his, but she still held herself in restraint.

"Come on, baby, kiss me back."

"I don't want to," she said, and groaned.

"Yes, you do. And you know the way I want it. Kiss me like that."

When his tongue probed the seam of her lips, they opened like the fragile petals of a flower. Growling with satisfaction, he slipped his tongue between them. It pierced the sweet, wet hollow of her mouth, delicately plundering, electrifying her with each deft thrust.

His hands scaled down her arms until he loosely encircled her wrists. He lifted her arms to his shoulders and left them there when he pressed his open hands to her sides. He ran them up and down her ribs, seesawing in the indentation of her waist. The heels of his palms ground gently against the sides of her breasts.

He took a step closer, but when even that wasn't close enough to suit him, he put his arms around her waist, flattened his hands on the small of her back, and pulled her against him, nestling his body against hers.

She uttered a startled cry when she felt his hard arousal against the softest, most vulnerable part of her body. He rubbed against her with intimate suggestion. Her mind spun out of control. Instinctually she cuddled him between her thighs.

A low mating sound rumbled in his chest as he sent his tongue deeper into her mouth. At the same time, his hands caressed her derriere, cupping her warmly and bringing her harder and higher against him.

He tore his mouth free and pressed it hotly against her arching throat. "I'm burning," he rasped out. "And so are you. Let's put out this fire."

He tugged on her shirttail and pulled it from the waistband of her slacks. When she felt his hand on her bare stomach it seemed like a brand and alerted her to just how hot things had gotten. "James, no," she protested feebly.

"Oh, yes, baby." He unfastened the lowest button on her shirt.

Laura panicked. "No." She shoved against his chest hard enough for him to get the message. He blinked, but it took several moments before his eyes, which were foggy with desire, cleared.

"Why?" His thick brows were drawn into a deep V. "You want it."

She shook her head vehemently. "No. I want to talk to you."

"Talk?" Reaching out, he curled a strand of her hair around his finger. He wiped the moisture of their kiss from her lips with it. "I like the way you . . . converse."

"No, James, listen to me. I wanted to tell you today that I'm leaving. The day after tomorrow if possible." She ignored his surprised expression and rushed on. Now that she had started, she wanted to finish, get it all out before she could be dissuaded. "There's no reason for me to stay now that the matter of the furnishings has been settled. I can be packed and ready to go within a couple of days."

"Where are you going?" His face was dark and intense.

"I—I'm not sure yet. But you and Mandy should assume occupancy right away. Where is she, by the way?"

"I have a lady in town who keeps her while I'm out."

Laura would have thought Mrs. Paden was caring for her granddaughter, but she didn't pursue the subject. She didn't have time. Because no sooner had she thought of the question than all thoughts were wiped from her mind, when he said, "I want you to stay."

"Stay?" Her voice had no more strength than her body.

"Yeah, as a housekeeper."

Her back stiffened and her chin went up several notches. "I'm not reduced to *that*, Mr. Paden." She would have gone around him, but he caught her arm and pressed her against the wall again.

"Hear what I have to say before you go huffing out. I don't mean housekeeper in the sense of cleaning and cooking. I've already made other arrangements for that."

"Housekeeping is an honorable profession. I merely meant that I didn't want to work for you."

"How do you know? I haven't told you what I had in mind." When she only stared back at him with cold condescension, he pressed on. "I need you as a *keeper* of Twenty-two Indigo Place. A hostess of sorts. A housekeeper will know what to clean, but will she know when to change the flower arrangements in the rooms and what kinds of flowers to use? I need someone to choose the china for dinner parties and plan menus and things like that. Understand now?"

"Yes, I understand, but the idea is ridiculous.

That kind of job would hardly keep me occupied. All pretense aside, I need a full-time, *paying* job."

"I intend to pay you."

"How much?" He told her, and she was flabbergasted by the amount. "Just for arranging flowers and selecting china?"

"And doing correspondence and helping me with Mandy. I can think of a thousand things."

"Well, I can't. I wouldn't have nearly enough to do to warrant that kind of salary."

He pushed back an unruly lock of hair with an impatient hand. "Look, I'm offering you a job, a job you'd be damned good at. It would be good for both of us. I need you and I know you need the job."

Her breath escaped her lungs slowly. She closed her eyes. Fury and humiliation warred within her, but the former got the upper hand. She wanted to lash out at him. Instead, when she finally opened her eyes and spoke, her words were controlled, but vibrating with loathing.

"Don't you dare pity me." All the pride of her ancestors was behind her. "I don't need largesse from you or anybody. I certainly don't want to either work for or take charity from a *Paden*."

He hooked his thumbs into the waistband of his jeans and studied her with smoldering eyes. He pulled his lower lip out from between his teeth. "Okay. How would you feel about marrying one?"

Six

"M—marry one? Marry you?"

He bobbed his head once. "Yeah, marry me."

"But that's preposterous!"

"Why?"

"A million reasons!" Laura spread her arms wide, as though to encompass them all.

"We're two single, consenting adults. That's all it takes for two people to get married."

Reasonable as that might sound, the idea was still so ridiculous that she was speechless. He, however, was armed with an arsenal of arguments.

"Hear me out, Laura, please, before you give me your final answer." He paused to collect his thoughts. For the first time, Laura could envision him in the role of businessman. In this mood, he commanded attention.

"I'm not kidding myself about how I'll be welcomed here in Gregory. I came back to town with my pockets lined with money, but there are lots of things it can't buy, as you so bluntly pointed out to me a few days ago." His mouth lifted into a brief grin. "I left town a black sheep, a misfit. That's how my name is emblazoned on everyone's memory. It will take years for that to change, if it ever does."

She started to interrupt, but he held up both hands for silence. "As you probably know, I don't give a damn what anybody thinks about me, but I sure as hell won't let them cold-shoulder Mandy just because she's my daughter. I can't guarantee her a respectable position in the community, but you can. Having Laura Nolan as a stepmother would get Mandy into just about any circle. I despise those cliques, but they're a way of life in this town."

"Then why didn't you choose to live someplace else?"

He gave her a wry smile and shrugged. "This is home." He took both her hands and pressed them between his. "If breaching those closed little groups is the only way to insure Mandy a good social standing, then that's what I'm going to do. I don't want her sitting out parties, like I had to."

Laura had the grace to look guilty. "If that's all you want, I could help by introducing—"

He shook his head emphatically. "My daughter needs a mother, Laura. I can't continue to be both parents. I never made the honor roll, but I'm smart enough to know that. She needs a woman's influence. And the older she gets, the more important that becomes."

"You could hire somebody, as you did before."

He tossed off her feeble suggestion with a negligent wave of his hand. "That's no good." He peered at her closely. "Do you think you could grow to like her?"

"Like Mandy? James, she's adorable. Of course I like her, and I'm sure in just a while I'd love her to distraction. But there's much more involved here."

"Like what?"

She stared at him with exasperation. "Like, for instance, you and I have nothing in common. Like you might fall in love with someone else. Like I might."

He frowned. "You aren't in love with anyone else, are you?"

"No." *I'm in love with you,* she thought. *And it breaks my heart that you're proposing marriage to me like a business transaction.* "It just wouldn't work, that's all."

"Isn't keeping Twenty-two Indigo Place worth a few sacrifices?"

Score one for you, she thought. But she wasn't ready yet to concede. "Asking me to spend the rest of my life with you hardly qualifies as 'a few sacrifices.'"

He braced his hand on the wall behind her head and leaned forward. "Am I so terrible?"

No. That was precisely the point. She wanted him to pledge undying love and consuming lust, but he was talking about a live-in governess, a hostess with social credentials. He wanted her to warm the community's attitude toward him and she wanted to warm his bed. "Out of this marriage you would get a mother for Mandy and the social endorsement of my family name."

"And you'd get to keep Indigo Place. A very fair bargain, I think. I'll throw in enough money to pay off the rest of your father's debts."

"I'm not a whore you can buy, James Paden."

He looked genuinely remorseful. "I'm sorry. That was unforgivably tactless. I didn't mean to imply that you are for sale. You see, Laura, I, as well as my daughter, need your tutelage. I've done well in business. I learned to play hardball with the big guys. I've cleaned up my language—most of the time—and my table manners. But I'm still igno-rant when it comes to social graces. Teach me."

"I can't think." Groaning, she pressed her tem-ples with her fingertips. "This is so—"

"Sudden? I know. At least to you it is. I've been thinking about it for days."

"*Days!* Why not give us a few weeks, months?"

"Can't afford the time," he said, shaking his head. "Mandy starts kindergarten in the fall. I want everything settled by then."

Laura looked forlorn. "I don't know why I'm even talking about this. It makes no sense."

"It makes perfect sense. Say yes."

"We're practically strangers."

"We've known each other for years."

"But not with any degree of . . . of . . ."

"Intimacy." He verbalized the word she was hav-ing such difficulty with.

"Yes." She lowered her head until her chin was almost touching her chest. "Would this be solely an 'arrangement' or would you expect me to be an actual wife to you?" Her heart was hammering so hard it hurt her chest.

Placing his finger beneath her chin, he raised her head and tilted it back until she had to look up at him. "Do you think I'd marry any woman with-out expecting her to share my bed?"

Her lips were trembling so drastically she couldn't answer. She merely shook her head. His eyes homed in on her damp, tremulous lips. "I can't wait to get you beneath me in bed," he whis-pered roughly. "When I do, I'm gonna give you the best time you ever had, Miss Laura." Softly, she gasped. "Say yes."

"I—"

He pressed a hot, fierce, brief kiss on her mouth,

then withdrew. "I won't take no for an answer. Say yes."

He kissed her in earnest then, lightly grinding his lips against hers until they parted. The deep, drugging kiss robbed her of her reasoning powers. She submitted to the dictatorship of his mouth.

He practiced no restraint, but kissed her as though she were the last woman on earth and he were under a deadline. He kissed her with primitive freedom, as if no rules of any society applied. Her lips were throbbing when he finally released them.

"Well?"

"Yes."

"Say it."

"Yes, I—I'll marry you, James."

"You'll become a Paden?"

She nodded, her lips already eagerly reaching up for his and another kiss. She wasn't disappointed. If his tongue was undisciplined before, it was savage now as it plunged into her mouth. She melted against him, feeling boneless and malleable and more womanly than ever in her life. His manliness demanded femininity from her. He coaxed it from every pore.

While keeping her mouth a willing participant in a thoroughly carnal kiss, he finished unbuttoning her blouse. Reaching beneath it in back, he unfastened her bra. He slid his hands around her sides and under the loosened garment until he cupped her full, warm breasts.

"God, I've been dying to do this," he said in her ear with a growl. His open mouth inched down her neck while his hands familiarized themselves with her breasts. "You've been driving me crazy. Crazy." He moaned as his fingertips feathered over the dainty tips.

Laura made a whimpering sound of longing and shame when her nipples tightened against the delicious pressure he applied. Her femininity felt warm and full and moist. For the first time in her life she wanted a man to fill her.

"That's right, baby. Hum for me now. Because when I get inside you, our bodies are going to sing. That's a promise." James dipped his knees slightly and nuzzled her breasts with his open mouth. His hands caressed the backs of her thighs, parting them marginally, so that when he straightened up, his manhood was wedged in the soft, yielding notch.

"James!" Laura was thrilled, but alarmed, at the stunning contact.

His fervency mellowed immediately to tenderness. He soothed her comfortingly. "Shh, shh." He ran his hands through her hair and pressed his lips against her cheek, breathing heavily, until both had regained their equilibrium. "Don't worry. I don't want our first time to be in a barn. I want a bed. A wedding bed. With you in it." He put space between them and gently pulled her blouse together over her breasts. "I had a wife, but that was only a legal term." He framed her face with his palms and gazed down at her. "You'll be my bride."

Once the wheels were set in motion, there was no stopping James, who had the momentum of a steamroller. Apparently he had given their marriage even more thought than he had confessed to. Otherwise the arrangements wouldn't have clicked off with the rhythm of a ticker tape.

He called Laura later that same afternoon to inform her that the wedding would take place on

Saturday in the courthouse. That gave her less than a week to prepare herself.

Early the next morning a familiar pickup truck clattered to a halt in the curved driveway in front of the house. Even before her husband, Bo, had a chance to assist her, Gladys got out and puffed up the steps of the front porch to embrace Laura, who had watched their unannounced arrival with open-mouthed amazement.

"Oh, I'm so glad to see you," she cried. "But what are you doing here so early in the morning?"

"Coming back to work, that's what," Gladys said.

"Coming back—"

"Mr. Paden hired us back, and not a minute too soon, I reckon," Gladys said with affected querulousness. "No telling what my kitchen looks like." She pulled an apron from her enormous handbag and tied it around her thick waist.

"Bo, are you gonna stand there grinning like a 'possum all day or are you gonna move our stuff back into the quarters and start getting this yard in shape? Lordy, Lordy, look at that flower bed.

"Let's go inside, lamb." She placed a possessive arm around Laura's shoulders. "Get out of this heat. I'll fix you some breakfast. You're skinnier than a willow sapling. I'll bet you haven't eaten a decent meal since your Gladys left."

With customary bossiness Gladys reestablished herself as housekeeper. When she happened to glimpse tears in Laura's eyes, she expressed immediate concern and took the younger woman in her smothering embrace. "No, nothing's wrong," Laura assured her. "It's just that I'm so glad to have you and Bo back."

"There, there, lamb, now, hush your crying. We're gonna take care of you, just like we promised your daddy. And I've got a new baby to spoil in that Mandy Paden. She reminds me of you when you were that age."

Having the Burtons back relieved Laura of the responsibility of running the household. The negative effect was that it gave her more time to ruminate about her pending marriage to James Paden.

During the ensuing days it became official. She was actually going to marry him. Laura had hoped there would be no more than a discreet mention of their forthcoming marriage on the society page. As it turned out, the newspaper ran a full-scale article about them. She was portrayed as no less than the glamorous reigning belle of Gregory society, while James was depicted as a returning conquering hero.

He laughed over the effusive story, recalling the time someone had written an editorial about the "vandalism" in the high school. "It was when me and some of my buddies drunkenly decided that the Confederate cannon in front of the courthouse would look better painted pink."

"You actually did that?" Laura exclaimed, laughing in recollection of the civic outrage the incident had prompted. They were sitting on the porch of Indigo Place in the wicker glider. Mandy was with Gladys in the kitchen, "helping" her bake tea cakes. "You were alleged to have done it, but I thought that might just be gossip."

"We used washable paint." He sounded repentant, but then winked in a way that made Laura think he'd do the prank again, given half a chance.

"You're a bad boy."

"I certainly am." He drew her close for a sexy kiss. "And I'm going to make you bad too," he promised with an affectionate snarl.

That was what she was afraid of. Since she had

accepted his proposal, he never let pass an opportunity to kiss or caress her. Each of those kisses left her tingling with desire. And while she liked the sensation, she was afraid of it.

Publicly the town was taking the prodigal to its bosom, but Laura wasn't fooled by this seeming change of heart. In the minds of Gregorians, James would always be that wild Paden kid. Now that she was going to be that wild Paden kid's wife, she was the object of sidelong glances of speculation, the kind the girls who went to the drive-in movie with him used to get.

Laura held her head up proudly, and coolly acknowledged congratulations on her marriage. Inside a mischievous imp was wanting to say, "Yes, his kisses are all they're purported to be and more. You should be so lucky."

If the social mavens in town were curious about the relationship between the bride and groom, they were positively rabid with jealousy over the marquis diamond that weighed down Laura's left hand with six and a half carats.

"But, James, this is—I can't—Why . . ." When he slipped the ring on her third finger all she could do was sputter.

"It reminded me of you," he said, staring into her eyes. "It's cool and smooth on the outside, but has lots of fire deep inside."

"But it's so . . . big." The last word was spoken in a weak voice. He was nibbling around her ear.

"Baby, I can't wait to fan your fire."

Her arms folded loosely around his neck and she gave herself up to his tempestuous kiss. "Where are we going to sleep?" He mumbled the question against her lips when he pulled away slightly.

"When?" she inquired groggily, half thinking he was wanting to haul her off to bed right then.

He chuckled. "When we get married."

"Oh!" Blushing hotly, she pushed away from him and made an ineffectual effort to straighten her hair. "I don't know what I was thinking."

"Bet I do." Wearing a lazy smile, he strummed the backs of his knuckles over her breasts. "And I like the idea. A lot. But I want to wait until Saturday night. I want to savor the thought of you. Besides, I'm afraid Gladys would whip me if I made a wrong move toward her lamb."

Laura shivered with the sensations his caressing fingers elicited, but forced her mind to focus on the question he had broached. "Mandy will take over my bedroom, won't she?"

"I think that's a fair guess. She calls it the Princess Room," he said with a grin he reserved for his daughter. "Anyway, it's too small for both of us, don't you think?"

"I suppose so. And there's a fireplace in the master suite. That might be nice on cold winter nights."

"For atmosphere. We won't need it for heat."

"No, the house has year-round air conditioning."

"That wasn't what I was talking about either." His arms went around her and pulled her against him as he bent his head low for another lengthy kiss.

Laura tried not to think about that kiss the next day as she began, with Gladys's help, preparing the master suite for a newly married couple to inhabit. Since her mother's death, the bedroom and adjoining dressing area and bath had taken on the ambiance of a bachelor's quarters. Randolph Nolan had left his stamp on the rooms.

Without robbing her old bedroom of any of its "princess" charm, Laura moved some of her personal belongings into the master suite. She installed new linens on the bed and towels in the bathroom. She and Gladys were pleased with the results. The suite now had a softer look and feel. The word "romantic" came to Laura's mind, but she shoved it aside.

The day before the wedding, James and Mandy officially moved in, bringing very little with them except their clothes, books, records, and Mandy's toys. He had sold all their furniture with the house in Atlanta.

By nightfall, everyone was agreeably tired. Mandy complained of having to spend another night in the hotel, but James promised that it would be the last one. His good-night kiss left Laura breathless and weak-kneed.

"Later," he said gruffly when he finally released her.

The bride had very little to do the following morning except to dread the hours before the ceremony and to "make yourself beautiful," as Gladys said.

In fact, had it not been for Gladys's solid presence at her side at the top of the stairs, issuing encouragement, she might not have walked down them to meet James when he arrived to drive her downtown.

"What have I done?" she kept asking herself.

But when she entered the judge's chambers with him and they began to recite their vows, she knew why she had accepted his proposal. She loved him. She wanted to live with him. That she would live with him in Indigo Place was an added bonus, an almost insignificant bonus, she realized as she turned toward him at the conclusion of the short ceremony.

"Hello, baby," he whispered. His clothing was correct, his behavior above reproach. But underneath the decorum befitting the solemn occasion, she saw the man, wild and undisciplined and dangerous, an enticing temptation to "nice girls" like Laura Nolan. The kiss he planted solidly on her mouth certainly didn't bow to convention. It went on forever, until the judge diplomatically cleared his throat.

Only Gladys, Bo, and Mandy had been there to witness the nuptials. Laura had tentatively asked James earlier in the week if his mother would be in attendance, but he had brusquely told her no. She had wisely let the subject drop.

After they left the courthouse, James insisted on treating them to supper and champagne in a private dining room he had reserved in the fanciest restaurant in town.

By the time they returned to Indigo Place, Laura had a roaring headache. Her nerves were raw. James must have sensed it. He came up behind her as she was helping Mandy unpack her last suitcase. He placed his hands tenderly on Laura's shoulders and said, "I'm paying Gladys to do chores like this. Go on to our room and relax. I'll be there shortly."

"But Mandy—"

"I'll see that she gets to bed." He kissed the back of Laura's neck. "Get out of this dress. It's beautiful and you look great in it, but I'm sure you can find something more . . . comfortable . . . to slip into. If you'll pardon the cliché."

She kissed her new daughter good night, thanked Gladys and Bo, who was bringing up the remainder of James's bags, and bade them all a good night.

After swallowing two aspirin, she bathed, hoping the soothing warm water would calm her serrated nerves. She spent a long time in front of the mirror in the dressing room, brushing her hair, applying lotion until her skin was as smooth as silk, and dabbing scent onto places so scandalous it made her blush. Primed for a wedding night, she went around the room lighting fragrant candles and, finally, turned down the bed.

Her efforts were rewarded. When James entered the room, he stood still on the threshold for several moments before softly closing the door behind him. He looked surprised and pleased.

Laura, standing in the middle of the room, nervously wringing her hands, asked, "Is Mandy all right?"

"She's asleep. She talked Gladys into singing her a lullaby. Gladys almost fell asleep before Mandy did." He chuckled as he shrugged out of his dark suit coat. He looked wonderful in his tailored vest. It hugged his trim torso, tapering to his waist.

He dropped his jacket onto the chaise, which Laura had moved into the bedroom. She picked up his coat and carried it into the dressing area. He followed her, unbuttoning the neat row of buttons on his vest. She hung up his coat and reached for the vest when he slung it down on the dressing-table stool.

"What are you doing?" He caught her hand in mid-action, as she reached for a hanger.

"Hanging up your clothes."

He yanked the vest from her hand and heedlessly tossed it to the floor. "That's right admirable of you, to do such a wifely task, *but*"—he ducked his head to nuzzle her neck—"I can think of other marital duties I'd rather you got busy with."

He swept her up into his arms and against his chest. She clutched the front of his shirt for balance as he carried her into the bedroom. His face was intense as he stared into hers. He set her down at the side of the bed.

"Did I tell you what a beautiful bride you were?" She shook her head, sending her hair brushing across the fingers that were caressing her neck.

He made a tsking sound. "Shame on me. You were—are—very beautiful. Your dress fit you perfectly." His eyes ranged down her body, taking in the pastel blue lace-and-silk negligee. "But I like you better like this," he said thickly.

He pressed his mouth to hers. Their lips parted. Their tongues touched. As the kiss deepened, he slipped the lacy robe off her shoulders. It slid to the rug at their feet. Laura shuddered with pleasure as his hands lightly coasted over her body, stopping frequently to investigate a curve, appreciate a hollow.

When he raised his head, he looked at her breasts through the sheer cups that supported them. His eyes narrowed, and he moaned. "Lord, you make me—"

He clenched his teeth, made a hissing sound, and squeezed his eyes shut. Groping for her hand at her side, he found it and carried it forward, pressing it over the front of his trousers.

Laura paled, then blushed hotly. But James didn't see, because his eyes were still closed and he was devotedly concentrating on the deliciousness of having her fingers folded around him. He chanted words and phrases that shocked her and made her tremble. "That's good, so good," he murmured, verbally titillating his wife.

After several moments, he opened his eyes and sighed deeply, giving her a chagrined smile. He let go of her hand and it dropped away from his body. "I want us to go slow. And I won't be able to take my time if we do too much of that."

She nodded wordlessly, unsure that she would ever have the power of speech again. She stood as still as a statue as he reached for the buttons of his shirt and undid them. He peeled the garment off with dispatch and it went the way of her robe. Leaving her standing, he sat down on the edge of the bed to take off his shoes and socks. Laura, it seemed, couldn't do anything without being coached. It was as though she had lost the capacity to think on her own, much less execute any voluntary action.

James unbuckled his belt and unsnapped his pants, but that was as far as he got. His eyes, never venturing too far away from the enticing picture her breasts made in the provocative nightgown, moved up to her face. "I can't even get undressed for wanting to have my hands on you," he remarked on a soft laugh.

He lightly squeezed her waist between his hands and drew her forward to stand at the edge of the bed between his wide-spread thighs. He rubbed his face against her breasts. Then his parted lips moved across them. His tongue touched her through the lace. His hands slid downward from her waist to her hips, then behind her, caressing and pressing, inching her closer to him.

"You smell good. I remember wanting to get close enough to smell you. I didn't think anbody could be as clean and fresh as Miss Laura Nolan looked. But you are." Making a sound of profound desire, he burrowed his nose in her cleavage, which was emphasized by the snug fit of her nightgown.

There was a row of pearl buttons down the front of the nightgown. They were more decorative than functional, because the gown could be easily slipped on and off without undoing them. But James chose now to unfasten them one by one. He did so slowly, pausing after each one to pay homage to the bit of flesh it revealed. As the buttons popped free of their fragile casings, her breasts swelled between the spreading wedge of lace, until they were fully revealed.

Laura had had no concept of just how seductive a man's mouth could be. She watched James's moving from one of her breasts to the other. She saw the questing motions of his lips, the flexing of his cheeks, the limber movements of his tongue. Then the pleasure they delivered became overwhelming, and her eyes slid shut. He left her very wet. The air cooled her as his head moved down. He kissed her tummy and each rib.

More buttons fell away under his nimble fingers. He peeled the straps of her nightgown from her shoulders and followed its slithering progress down her body with his hands. The gown pooled around her feet, but he didn't even give her an opportunity to step out of it.

He kissed her navel. Lower. He kissed places where Laura didn't know kissing was permissible.

She was adrift in an ocean of feelings, all new, all untried, all glorious. Her fingers were knotted in his hair, mindlessly clutching at the silky strands. When his hands pressed her derriere forward and urged her closer yet to his caressing mouth, she arched her back and obliged him without thinking about it.

Not until he gently pulled her down onto the bed, and lowered himself to partially cover her, did her reason return. She lifted slumberous blue eyes to the green intensity of his. His breathing was barely controlled, and struck her face in warm gusts.

"I want you." Without releasing her from his hot gaze, he slipped his hand down to his fly and unzipped it. Laura stared up at him with the fascination of a doe caught in the hunter's sight. The rasp of his zipper was followed by the rustling sound of fabric against skin as he shoved his trousers down his legs and kicked them free. He lay one hard thigh over hers.

"Get ready. I'm going to kiss you like I've always wanted to." His voice was rough, deep, aggressive.

His mouth came down hard and forcefully, but she was waiting for it. His tongue roughly parted her lips, but when he thrust it into her mouth, her lips closed around it and sucked it deeper inside. Her nails dug into the supple muscles of his back.

He wedged his knee between her thighs and levered his body over one side of hers so she could feel the full extent of his arousal. He rubbed himself against her thigh. The sounds emanating from his hair-dappled chest were yearning, hungry sounds.

He left her lips rosy and moist and lowered his mouth to her breasts. His fervent kisses were tempered only by his desire to give her as much pleasure as he took. His tongue was agile and playful. It indulged his every whim and fulfilled her every fantasy.

One of his hands smoothed down the outside of her thigh to her knee. He cupped the back of it and lifted it to stroke the sensitive underside of her thigh. Up, up, toward the source of the heat that consumed her.

Her reaction to his touch was violent, but splendid. Her back arched off the bed and she gave a sharp cry of sheer ecstasy. He, breathing heavily and hardly able to restrain himself from taking her immediately, circled the mouth of her femininity with his fingertip. Laura plaintively sighed his name and clutched his shoulders. James explored inside. Stroking the softness. Probing the wetness. Deeper.

A heartbeat later, he was sitting on the edge of the bed, his head resting on his hands, his elbows propped on his knees. His breathing was labored, and filled the romantically beautiful bedchamber with a discordant thrashing sound.

Laura, one arm folded across her eyes, the other lying palm up, helpless and vulnerable at her side, bit her lower lip to keep him from hearing her weeping.

"Why didn't you tell me?"

"I don't understand. Tell you what?"

"Tell me that you were a virgin."

"I . . ." She tried to moisten her mouth by swallowing, but it didn't help. "I thought you knew."

"Well, I didn't."

Angrily he came off the bed and crossed the room in long strides. Startled by his sudden movement, Laura jumped. He went to the antique portable tea cart that served as a liquor cabinet. Laura had thought it would add a homey touch to the room and had never considered that it would actually be functional. But James lifted the stopper out of a crystal decanter and splashed a generous shot of bourbon into a highball glass. He downed the whiskey in two swallows.

Wary of his temper, she pulled the sheet up to her chin, hiding her nakedness. Her breasts still bore the faint scratches of his beard stubble, and she was certain her mouth looked well-kissed. It felt well-kissed. As for the rest of her body, it was still pulsing with unrequited arousal.

"Does my virginity make a difference?" she asked tremulously.

"A difference?" He spun around. "Hell, yes, it makes a difference."

Laura was momentarily mesmerized by the sight of him. Spared from being completely naked only by his briefs, he looked fierce and masculine and supremely virile. His passion hadn't been totally squelched, she noted, glancing down his body to where his shorts were stretched in front.

His skin was one toasty tan color all over. His body hair was light brown and gilded by the summer sun. It grew darker only in that dense patch that swirled around his navel.

"Why?" She was sincerely bewildered by this sudden and volatile mood shift and the apparent reason behind it.

He raked a hand through his hair, increasing the tousled condition her hands had already caused. He was seemingly impervious to his unclothed state and the havoc it was causing his bride.

"Don't you realize the responsibility a man assumes when he takes a woman's virginity?"

Laura looked up at him with wide-eyed misapprehension and shook her head. He cursed vividly and poured himself another two fingers of bourbon. He tossed the drink down his throat and set the glass on the tea cart with enough emphasis to rattle the other glassware.

He went around the room blowing out the candles, then came toward the bed with a belligerent swagger. A deep frown was creasing his brows. His mouth was as sullen as a young boy's whose favorite kite just got tangled up in a tree.

He shoved his thumbs into the waistband of his briefs. "Have you ever seen a naked man?"

Laura swallowed hard and shook her head. "Only in magazines."

He cursed again, less loudly, but more crudely. "Well, brace yourself."

She tried, but he didn't give her much time. It wouldn't have mattered. Nothing could have prepared her for James. He was still partially aroused. But rather than being frightened or repulsed, as he seemed to think she would be, she was intrigued and excited and curious—and desperately disappointed when he switched out the light.

She felt the mattress give with his weight as he settled down beside her. He pulled the sheet over himself and turned his back to her.

Never had Laura felt so rejected. She lay rigid in the darkness, trying not to shake the bed as she cried. Tears slid down her cheeks in streams. Unable to control them, she sniffed.

James turned over. "Laura?" When she answered with a soft hiccupping sob, he mumbled another curse, but scooted toward her and put his arm around her shoulders. "Don't. Don't cry. I'm not mad at you."

"I thought husbands wanted their wives to be virgins. I never thought you'd be turned off by it."

He was far from turned off, but he didn't tell her that. "This has nothing to do with you," he said, sifting her hair through his fingers. "I just never counted on being the guy to deflower Miss Laura Nolan, that's all."

"Mrs. Laura Paden," she whispered in the dark.

He smiled. And at the risk of breaking his control, he leaned over and kissed her gently on the temple.

Seven

Sitting on the pier, his bare feet dangling over the water, James called himself every foul name he could think of. When he had exhausted that list, he started making up names. When his imagination ran out, he began enumerating all the kinds of fool he was.

Last night he had had a beautiful woman in his bed. Naked and willing. A beautiful, naked, and willing woman who was also his wife. And, like an idiot, he hadn't made love to her. For the first time since his loss of innocence at the tender age of thirteen with an experienced girl of eighteen who had made the first move, James Paden had been incapable of taking a woman.

Not physically incapable. Hell, no, not physically. Physically, he was still ready. Several times during the night he had awakened, hard and aching with want. Beside him Laura lay sleeping. He could smell her, feel her warmth, hear her soft breathing.

At daybreak, disgusted and furious with himself, he had thrown off the covers and clandestinely left the bedroom without waking his wife. Dressing only in a pair of cut-offs he had soundlessly taken from a bureau drawer, he went outside.

The morning was humid and still. The muggy air was heavily scented with gardenia and honeysuckle that grew wild in the woods surrounding 22 Indigo Place. Sunlight filtered through the mist that hovered over St. Gregory's Sound, as yet to be burned away.

Why? he asked himself. Why had finding her intact been such a stunning deterrent to him? He had ruminated on the question and had finally drawn some conclusions.

First, he had never had a virgin before, for the very reason he had given Laura last night. He hadn't wanted to assume the responsibility. Strange that such a skirt-chaser as he had had any qualms about that, but he always had.

He had never hesitated to further a woman's bad, or even questionable, reputation, but he had scruples against compromising a woman for the first time. He also grew squeamish at the thought of inflicting pain. Sex had been nothing but pure pleasure for him . . . ever. He hated to think that his partner wasn't deriving at least some satisfaction from it.

But she's your wife! he argued with himself.

Still, being Laura Nolan's first lover carried awesome obligations with it. He wasn't sure he could live up to them. It galled him that he felt inferior, but he had to admit that that was at the crux of his hesitation.

If people labelled you "trash" long enough, eventually you started believing they were probably right. He and Laura couldn't have been more diametrically opposite. In the eyes of the world, they were totally unsuited to each other. She was from one of the most aristocratic families in Georgia. He was trash. Deeply seated inside him was the notion that he really *wasn't* good enough for her.

He cursed, kicked up a spray of water, and then came to his feet. He stamped along the pier toward the shore, his shoulders hunched defensively.

Hadn't he proved to the world by now that one could overcome his background if he set his mind to it? Hadn't his fame and fortune bought him invitations into the homes of the South's most prominent families? What the hell was he trying to prove to these crackers in Gregory?

He had lived down his past, putting it all behind him, divorcing himself from it. He didn't even claim his own mother, short of sending her a generous allowance every month. Why should he feel inferior to anyone?

Yet it had scared him silly when Laura had looked up at him with such trust.

Because riding right up there on his shoulder with his inferiority complex was his guilt. He would hate to have her know that he had come back to Gregory with the intention of not only buying 22 Indigo Place, but of marrying her as well. His seemingly spontaneous proposal had been carefully blueprinted.

She *was* Indigo Place. They were one and the same. He had wanted them both, the whole package. Laura and the address represented everything he had always wanted and could never have . . . until now.

When his hired scouts had informed him that 22 Indigo Place was for sale, he had put his relocation plans into effect immediately. The timing couldn't have worked out better. Mandy was due to start kindergarten when summer vacation was over. As expeditiously as possible, he had sold his house and furnishings in Atlanta, finalized the sale of his business, and prepared to put down roots in Gregory. Living in Indigo Place, having Laura Nolan as his wife, would open doors that had previously been closed to him.

But, he thought now as he slowed his determined march back toward the house, Laura Nolan hadn't been what he had expected. She was still pretty in that quiet, refined way. Her grooming and manners were still impeccable. She still spoke eloquently. She was unquestionably a lady.

But she was also a woman, and he hadn't counted on that. He had expected to woo her into marriage, emotionlessly consummate it, then settle into a dignified and amenable relationship that would benefit them both, but that wouldn't interfere with their private lives too much. He had imagined he would set up a mistress out of town, an obliging woman who would slake the lust his wife found base and repulsive.

It had come as a major shock to James to discover that the prim and proper girl of his memory experienced her own lust. Beneath her cool exterior, there smoldered a fire just waiting for the right man to come along and fan it to life. Laura had rid his mind of any plans for a mistress or extramarital affairs of any sort. If anyone slaked his lust, he wanted it to be his wife.

In the few days before their wedding, he'd been thinking much more about the wedding night than about having his goal within his grasp. Having Laura in his life had taken prominence over acquiring her social standing. His excitement over their marriage had disturbed him. It was downright scary to acknowledge that she was a woman worth cherishing, and not just a decorative trophy that represented his accomplishments.

Except for Mandy, he had never cared whether anyone loved him or not. He wanted Laura to love him.

"Daddy!" Mandy hollered from the back door, "Gladys says if you're not in here in two shakes, your breakfast will get cold."

He waved at his daughter and jogged the remainder of the way to the house. While he'd been brooding down at the pier, Gladys and Bo had begun their morning chores. Bo was already tilling the soil in the azalea beds. James could smell bacon cooking.

As soon as he entered the back door, Mandy handed him a clean T-shirt to pull on. He gave her a hearty good-morning hug and kiss and together they sat down at the breakfast table, which Gladys had heaped with food.

"When you get done, I'll fix a tray for you to carry up to Laura," the housekeeper told him as she refilled his coffee cup. "I reckon she's too tired to come down to breakfast this morning." Gladys gave him a broad wink. He smiled sickly into his plate of pancakes.

Making good her promise, Gladys prepared a tray for Laura. "Can I go wake her up, too, Daddy?" Mandy asked as James carried the tray from the kitchen.

"No, honey pie, you stay here with me. I might need some help," Gladys said.

"It's all right, Gladys." Actually James welcomed Mandy to act as a buffer between him and his chaste bride. "Laura didn't get to spend much time with Mandy yesterday. I'm sure she won't mind."

Mandy tore up the stairs in front of him, but at the door of the master suite he stopped her from charging in. "Let me go first," he suggested, remembering Laura's lack of sleeping apparel. When he had left her, one trim leg had been lying outside the covers and the pink tip of one breast had been peeking from beneath the sheet. "You stay here and guard the tray until I call you."

Mandy looked disappointed, but obeyed him as he set the heavy tray on a hall table. He opened the bedroom door cautiously and crept into the shadowed room. Going first to the windows, he opened the slats of the shutters to fill the room with sunlight.

He picked up Laura's robe and gown, which, in his large hands, amounted to no more than scraps of fabric and lace, and carried them into the dressing room. He exchanged them for a more modest robe and carried that back to the bed.

He lowered himself to the side. Asleep, Laura looked innocent and extremely young. Her brown, sun-lightened hair was in an endearing tangle around her face. It spilled over the pillow alluringly. He couldn't resist touching it, and rubbed a strand between his fingers. His eyes detailed her slender form beneath the sheet. Her shoulders were bare above it, as creamy and smooth as magnolia petals, and, he knew from experience, were just as fragrant.

The lace-edged hem of the sheet was still flirting with one nipple, rosy and flushed with sleepy warmth, every time she drew a breath. That flirtation had caused it to peak slightly. His loins tightened and, though he'd just eaten, he felt a gnawing akin to hunger inside him.

"Laura." Her name sounded so agreeable on his tongue. He hadn't known until then that Laura was one of his favorite names. "Laura." He repeated her name as much for the pleasure of speaking it aloud as to awaken her.

Her eyelids lifted drowsily. "Hmm?"

"You have a very impatient stepdaughter waiting outside to say good morning to you."

She opened her eyes more fully. What greeted them brought her wide awake. James's lap. Covered in tight, soft denim that gloved his sex.

Shoving her hair out of her face, she sat up, flustered, dragging the sheet with her. "Good morning."

"Hi."

Laura wondered then if the sex appeal he exuded was intentional or if it was something that came naturally. Was it just as much a part of him as his green eyes and pouty lower lip?

He always emanated a raw masculinity that hinted that he was either thinking about sex or planning it or remembering it. It mattered not if he was dressed in suit and tie, shorts and T-shirt, or was naked. He called to mind a predator on the prowl, but one confident of catching and quelling his prey. There was an inherent restlessness about him that appealed to every woman and made her want to be the one who finally assuaged that constant hunger within him.

"Hungry?"

Laura glanced at him quickly. Had he read her mind? "Yes. I think I am."

"Good. Gladys cooked you a breakfast fit for a lumberjack. Do you mind if Mandy and I visit with you while you eat it?"

"I'd like that."

"I'll call her in. But maybe you'd better slip this on first." He held out the robe he had brought from the dressing room. Since he offered her no choice,

Laura let go of the sheet. It slipped to her waist, leaving her breasts bare.

James helped guide her arms into the sleeves of the robe, but when she automatically reached for the buttons, he pushed her hands aside.

Slowly he did up the buttons and carefully tied the ribbon that was threaded through the casing beneath her breasts. His knuckles bumped into the soft mounds. Both pretended not to notice.

When he was finished, he sat back and looked at her with satisfaction. He tucked a loose strand of hair behind her ear. "There, perfect."

Then, just because he couldn't resist it, he cupped her breast and pushed it up until it swelled over her modest neckline. He bent his head and placed his mouth against the smooth flesh, blessing it with a lingering kiss.

Laura was so overcome by the tender gesture, she could barely find enough voice to speak when James opened the door moments later and Mandy came rushing in. She jumped into the middle of the bed and greeted Laura with an enthusiastic kiss.

"Is this where Daddy slept?" she asked, plumping up the extra pillow beside Laura.

"Yes," Laura said, nervously cutting her eyes up at James, who was placing the breakfast tray over her lap.

"Just like on TV," Mandy said, beaming a smile.

"TV?" Laura sipped the coffee James had considerately poured for her before sitting down on the edge of the bed again. His hip was propped against hers.

"On TV there's always a mommy and a daddy and they always sleep in the same bed. But I didn't have a mommy, so my daddy always had to sleep by himself. Now he doesn't. I'm glad you're my mommy now."

Laura set down her cup. Emotion was so thick in her throat, she would have been unable to swallow. "So am I, Mandy." She extended her arms to the child. Mandy launched herself against Laura and hugged her tight.

Over Mandy's head, she looked at James. He kissed his finger and laid the kiss on Laura's soft lips.

Their days fell into a routine of sorts. James was often on the telephone in the mornings and early afternoons. Laura suspected that he was doing just what he had said he was going to do: look for an interesting way to make his next million. Even in his youth he'd been wild, but never shiftless, never a laggard.

He discussed some of his investment ideas with Laura. She was astounded by his ambition. Nothing intimidated him. He dismissed obstacles left and right. He made the most outlandish ideas sound feasible. The correspondence he received from respected industrialists indicated that she wasn't the only one who thought his ideas were practical and workable.

They made frequent trips into town. Laura got over her skittishness at being seen with James and adjusted to playing the role of mother to Mandy. She basked in the enjoyment of being part of a family. She wasn't impervious to the appreciative glances cast in James's direction and took a secret, almost smug, satisfaction in being the woman on his arm.

People spoke to them cordially, but socially James still wasn't fully accepted. Everyone was in awe of his wealth, but no one was quite willing to accept him into the fold. He never mentioned it, but Laura knew this greatly disturbed him, more for Mandy's sake than his own.

"James," she ventured one evening. They were sitting in the front parlor. Mandy had fallen asleep with her head in Laura's lap while Laura was reading her a story. James was perusing the *Wall Street Journal.*

"Hmm?"

"Why don't we give a party?"

He tipped the corner of the paper down. "A party?"

"It's been a long time since a party has been held at Twenty-Two Indigo Place—long before Father died."

"What did you have in mind?"

He asked the question with almost hostile gruffness, but she could tell he was interested. "Oh, something casual with lots of people and live music. While the weather is still warm. We could open up all the doors so the guests could meander outside. Maybe string lanterns in the trees and out onto the pier. Gladys and Bo would be thrilled to show the place off since you've made so many improvements. What do you think?"

He folded his newspaper, laid it aside, and stared at her for a lengthy moment. "Would this be a party for funsy's sake or do you have an ulterior motive?"

"What kind of motive could I have?"

"It would be a coming-out party for Mandy and me, wouldn't it?"

Laura steadily returned her husband's gaze. They had been married for several weeks, but she was still his wife in name only. She knew he wanted her. Often she caught him looking at her wistfully or with outright lust. The desire he couldn't mask reciprocated her own. They got along well during the day. They never lacked for something interesting or entertaining to talk about. Laughter was a part of most of their conversations.

But when they entered the bedroom each night, they became two different people, who were uneasy around each other. Tension was as thick as molasses. They undressed in silence. Once in bed, they would face each other. Always in the dark. He would caress her, never in erogenous places. Sometimes he would kiss her, but never for long and never passionately.

Laura's nerves were constantly on edge. Her skin itched beneath the surface, and no amount of scratching would ease it. She was wound up like a spring and was constantly on guard against breaking free.

She wanted to be possessed by her husband. It was as simple as that. She wanted to know the hard, demanding power of his body inside hers. Why he chose not to make love to her remained a mystery. Surely he didn't intend to keep her a virgin forever. By now he should have grown accustomed to the idea and worked it out in his mind. Perhaps he was waiting for an encouraging sign from her. Was this the opportunity she'd been waiting for to make her urgent desires known?

Tossing her hair back and looking at him boldly, she said, "I'm proud of you and Mandy. I want to show you off to my friends. I want everyone in town to know how glad I am to be your wife."

Lest she see how much her declaration affected him, James stood up abruptly and went to the window, keeping his back to the room. He wanted to say, "You'd do that for me? Why?" And he fantasized her saying back, "Because I love you."

But if he was anything, he was a realist. Life had taught him to be. He was afraid to force the issue with Laura because he was still ambivalent about his feelings toward her.

And what if, God forbid, he was reading her the wrong way? She just might be glad to be his wife because she now had a bottomless checking account.

She certainly hadn't squandered money, had even been reluctant to accept the checkbook he had given her. But he'd been around enough conniving women to be mistrustful of motives that seemed sincere. The fact remained that he had bailed Laura Nolan out of a jam. It might be that what he was seeing in her blue eyes every time she looked at him was nothing more than gratitude.

The last thing he wanted from her was gratitude. What man with guts and intelligence wanted gratitude from a lovely, sexy, vibrant woman? Not me! So when he answered, his voice held more annoyance than he intended. "Fine. Whatever you want to do."

Crestfallen over his lack of enthusiasm for her idea, Laura excused herself and took Mandy upstairs. That night when James joined her in bed, he turned away from her.

There were no caresses. There were no kisses. Not even in the dark.

Stubbornly Laura put her plans for the party into effect.

She ordered the invitations the following morning. A week later, as she sat pondering the guest list at the secretary in the parlor, James came striding in, his boot heels thudding heavily on the hardwood floors.

Bracing his arms on the back of her chair, he leaned over and read her list of things to order. At the side of that column, she had neatly made another of how much she had budgeted for each item. "Don't scrimp on anything. Let's do it up right, show these snooty Gregorians how it's done."

"Are you sure you want to give me carte blanche?" she asked teasingly, looking up at him. "I have expensive taste."

He kissed the tip of her nose lightly, then her lips. "Your expensive taste is one of the things I like best about you." When he smiled that insinuating smile, her insides melted. Her heart beat heavily. "Can you spare a minute?"

"Yes." There was a husky quality to her voice. She was hoping he might suggest that they go upstairs to bed.

Instead he took her hand. "Come outside. I have something to show you."

Hiding her disappointment, she let him lead her to the front door, which he opened with a flourish. His green eyes were dancing mischievously.

When Laura stepped through the door, her mouth fell open with surprise. Three horse trailers were parked end to end in the driveway. She recognized the horses being backed out of them.

"Those are . . . that's . . ." Tears welled in her eyes.

"Thought you might recognize them."

"Oh, James!" She turned to face him. "How did you find them?"

"Connections," he said with a lazy, conceited smile.

"James." She flung herself against him and wrapped her arms around his neck. Burying her face in the hollow of his throat, she hugged him hard. "Thank you," she whispered fiercely before releasing him and racing down the front steps to welcome home the horses that had been sold months before.

It would be difficult to determine who was the most excited that morning, Laura or Mandy, who became the ecstatic owner of a pony. The horses were walked into the stalls, which Bo had been secretly preparing for them. Mandy was outfitted with a saddle and received her first riding lesson from Laura. Only a promise from Laura that they would ride again the next day succeeded in bribing her out of the stable to take a bath before dinner.

Laura was giving her favorite mount a rubdown when James joined her in the shadowy barn. "Thank you again," she said.

"I liked the way you thanked me earlier better."

He was leaning against a support post, one knee bent, his foot propping him up. His eyes maintained their insolence, but she read the challenge in them. Dropping her currycomb, she moved out of the stall and went to stand directly in front of him and between his thighs. "You mean like this?" She folded her arms around his neck.

"Uh-huh." He linked his hands together behind her at her waist.

"Why did you do it?"

"What, buy the horses back?" When she nodded, he said, "Two reasons. I thought I might win a few points with you."

"You did. What's the second reason?"

"I like what your cute little butt does to a pair of ordinary blue jeans." He slid his hands into the seat pockets of her jeans and pulled her forward until her front was pleasantly complementing his.

"Thank you kindly, sir, but what does that have to do—"

"You ride horses, you wear jeans."

"Hmm, I get your drift."

"Move against me like that again, baby, and you'll get more than my drift."

He barely got the words out before he slanted his mouth over hers and kissed her soundly. But, unfortunately, before the kiss had a chance to develop into something more, they were interrupted.

"Excuse me, James, but there's a long distance call for you." Hat in hand, Bo stood hesitantly in the square of light at the stable door.

James's mutterings were obscene as he stalked from the stable.

After that, things became considerably more strained between them, rather than the reverse.

Laura had fully expected him to make love to her that night. Mentally and emotionally she prepared herself for it. She primped for an hour in the dressing area before sliding between the scented sheets of the master bed.

When James stayed downstairs talking business into the telephone long after she had retired, she felt humiliated and rejected. By the time he came upstairs, she had whipped her temper into a fine froth.

"Must you make so much racket when you tramp upstairs?" She lit into him the instant he closed their bedroom door. "Sherman's troops didn't make that much noise on their march across Georgia."

James had telephoned everybody in his address book while trying to decide if he had the finesse, the gentle technique, needed to make love to a virgin. He knew Laura had great expectations based upon his reputation as a lover without equal. He was touchy, to say the least. He had anticipated a limpid look and a soft touch, but got instead daggers and claws. He immediately took offense. "So sorry, madam, to have disturbed your beauty rest."

Laura flopped back down on the pillow. Animosity seethed between them when he got into bed. Not only were the caresses and kisses dispensed with, there weren't even any good nights spoken, though both lay awake for a long time.

The next day their tempers flared several times. The climate in the house was so turbulent whenever she and James shared a room, that Laura decided it would be prudent if they got away from each other for a while. She volunteered to run a few household errands for Gladys and took Mandy with her for company.

The hardware store was the last stop on their list. To get there, they had to pass the house where Leona Paden resided. On impulse, Laura wheeled into the narrow driveway and parked behind a modest recent-model car.

"Where are we going, Mommy?" Mandy asked.

The name Mandy used so naturally to address her never failed to bring a pleased smile to Laura's face. "To visit a lady. Be on your best behavior, okay?"

Laura had butterflies in her stomach as they alighted from the car. What she was about to do was risky. She was toying with something that was none of her business, but it bothered her tremendously that James ignored his mother's existence. She intended to right that wrong if at all possible.

The brick house was small, but tidy. The front sidewalk was bordered with periwinkles. Holding Mandy's hand, Laura rang the doorbell. Moments later the front door was opened by James's mother. The woman's shock couldn't have been affected. After a moment of stunned silence, she said, "Laura Nolan, isn't it?"

"Hello, Mrs. Paden. I didn't know whether you'd remember me or not."

"You're married to James now."

"Yes."

"I read about it in the paper. Would you like to come in?" Her hospitality was almost apologetic, and Laura's heart opened up to the woman she knew must have suffered terribly in her lifetime.

"I'd love to visit with you for a minute. If we wouldn't be a bother."

"Lordy, no." Mrs. Paden pushed open the screen door and moved aside so Laura and Mandy could step into a spotless living room. She looked down at Mandy and extended her hand toward the child, withdrawing it before she actually touched her. "Is this . . . ?" A tremor shook her, and she was unable to complete her question.

Laura answered it for her. "This is Mandy." She gave Mandy a gentle nudge forward.

It wasn't really necessary. The little girl's sweet personality prevailed. "Hello. My name is Mandy Paden, and this is Annmarie." She held up the doll that was never far from her. "Annmarie's my best friend. Except for Mommy and Daddy. Do you know my daddy?"

What ensued was one of the most emotionally wrenching hours Laura had ever spent in her life. She rarely knew whether to smile at Mandy's candid chatter or to cry over Mrs. Paden's visible greed to hear it. When she left, she embraced the older woman and made a promise. "We'll come again soon."

Mandy talked about her new friend all the way

home. When they pulled into the driveway, Laura said, "Mandy, about this afternoon, let's keep it a—"

"There's Daddy!"

Before Laura could caution Mandy to keep their visit to Mrs. Paden a secret, Mandy opened the car door and ran to meet James, who was descending the front steps. He swung her up in his arms and held her high over his head while she squealed in delight.

By the time Laura reached them, Mandy was babbling. "And she lived in a nice house, only not as big and pretty as Nindigo Place. She has hair that's kinda white and kinda brown and her eyes are green like yours and mine, 'cept more wrinkledy. She told me I could call her Grandma if I wanted to and gave me cookies. They were out of a box, but she said the next time I come to see her, she'll bake me some. And she has a picture of you on top of her TV, and you look real funny in it. It was before you grew whiskers, I think. She was real nice, only I think she's kinda sad because sometimes when she looked at me I thought she was going to cry. And she said she knew how to sew, and that she'd make me and Annmarie dresses alike. And . . ."

Mandy wound down when, with the keen perception of a child, she realized that her daddy wasn't sharing her enthusiasm for her new friend. In fact, he was wearing a face that was new to her. It reminded her of the bad men on TV.

"Gladys has cooked you a good lunch," he said, carrying her inside. "She'll get cross if we let your chicken noodle soup get cold."

He deposited his daughter at the table in the kitchen, where three place settings had been laid.

Gladys's welcoming smile faded when she noted the strained expression on Laura's face.

That James's temper was about to erupt became readily apparent. "Gladys, when Mandy finishes her lunch," he said in clipped tones, "I suggest you settle her down for a nap. She's had a busy morning."

"Aren't you going to eat?" Gladys asked with more courage than Laura could have garnered at the moment.

"No. Laura, I'd like to see you upstairs."

Just so there was no argument about it, he closed his fingers around her wrist, jerked her forward, and practically dragged her all the way to the master suite.

As soon as they entered the bedroom, he confronted her furiously. "I want to know what the hell you thought you were doing, taking my daughter to see *her*."

"Don't yell at me."

"Answer me!" he shouted.

"She's your mother, James."

"One of nature's cruelest jokes."

Laura shivered. "Your attitude toward her is deplorable. You should be ashamed of yourself."

"I send her money every month." His mouth was curled into an ugly smirk.

"Right," Laura said angrily. "I saw the new house and the new furniture, the car. Her clothes are certainly several grades above what she had to wear years ago. She's well fed and seems in good health. But I also saw her loneliness and despair. She was starved for someone to talk to. You should have seen her with Mandy. She—"

"You had no right to take my daughter there without my permission, Laura."

She ignored him. "I can't describe how loving

she was with your child. I could tell she wanted to crush Mandy against her and hold her tight."

"I don't want to hear it." He sliced the air with his hands.

"And each time your name was mentioned, she hung on to every word. Lying on the end table in her living room was the newspaper article about our marriage. It topped a stack of many such articles about you. They had been folded and refolded so many times, they were falling apart."

Tears ran from her eyes with the memory of that collection of newspaper clippings. It had been a pitiful sight. Impatiently she dashed her tears away with the backs of her fists, more angry than sad.

"How can you be so cruel, James? How can you so heartlessly shut your own mother out of your life?"

"It's my business," he ground out.

"I don't know what she did to make you so unforgiving, but surely—"

"Stay out of it. It doesn't concern you."

"It does! I'm your wife."

"Not quite." He slammed the door closed behind him. "But I'm gonna fix that right now."

Eight

"What are you going to do?" Laura took cautious steps backward.

"I'm going to make you my wife. Make you a woman." James lunged forward and gripped her upper arms.

"No!" She tried to wrest her arms free, but he was too strong.

"You wanna butt in where you don't belong?" He sneered. "Well, the place you belong *most* is in my bed."

He shoved her down on the bed. She landed on her back and tried to roll away, but he followed her down and trapped her beneath him. "Before you start handling my life, Mrs. Paden, you need to learn how to handle me."

"You're crude." Her blue eyes sparked with fury as she virtually spat the words out. "Let me go."

"Not a chance, baby."

"And stop calling me baby. I'm not one of your casual pickups."

"You're sure as hell not," he said, barking a short laugh. "Do you think I'd put up with your snottiness if you were? The one place putting on airs doesn't count is in bed. So far, Miss Laura, I've been remarkably unimpressed with you."

He claimed his rights to her mouth. Brutal lips ground against hers. He tunneled his fingers through her hair all the way to her scalp. Like a vise, his hands closed around her head and held it still for the plunder of his tongue.

Outraged, Laura squirmed beneath him and pounded his shoulders and back with her fists. The blows were ineffectual, but he soon tired of them and manacled both her wrists with one hand. Hauling her arms above her head, he stapled them to the bed with his hard fingers. Buttons went flying when he yanked on the front of her blouse. He tore open her brassiere with the same disregard. His free hand closed around her breast.

He felt her heartbeat against his palm. It telegraphed a vital message to his brain. His head snapped up. Bracing himself above her, he looked down into her face. Her labored breathing matched his, and what he saw in her face wasn't revulsion or fear, it was desire.

Again his mouth possessed hers. But this time his kiss had a different personality. It was just as hungry, just as savage, but far less rough. His tongue was rowdy and undisciplined, but not vicious. It gave pleasure rather than inflicted punishment.

Another emotion rose out of Laura's rage. From the cleft between her thighs, heat began to swirl in widening circles. She struggled for her arms to be freed, not to get away from him, but to participate in this stormy exchange of kisses. When he did release her hands, she plunged them into his hair, twining her fingers through it to hold his mouth against hers.

Groaning, he dipped his head and kissed her neck so ardently that he left faint bruises on her fragile skin. "I can't wait any longer, baby. I've got to have you. Now."

He wedged his hand between their bodies and lifted her skirt. She accommodated him, assisting by raising her hips when he slipped her panties down. He worked frantically with the zipper of his jeans to free himself. He was warm and hard. He placed the velvety tip of his sex against her. "Will I hurt you?"

"I don't know."

"Do you care?"

Her head thrashed from side to side. "No."

He entered her cautiously. Then, encouraged by the way her body yielded to him, he completed his possession with one swift stroke.

Gnashing his teeth against the ultimate sensation that engulfed him, James burrowed his head in the hollow of her shoulder. He gave her body time to adjust to the violation of his, but even the strictest self-imposed restraint couldn't prevent him from doing what nature had ordained. The rhythm of his thrusts increased until an explosive climax seized him.

He settled against Laura heavily, his breath a tempest in her ear. "Are you in pain, Laura?"

"No," she answered honestly. There was no pain, only a supreme dissatisfaction. Her body was still restless.

"I'm sorry." He kissed her ear.

"For what?"

Laughing softly, he raised his head and gazed down into her puzzled eyes. She still didn't know what she had missed. "My darling, innocent, highbrow girl." Affection shone from his eyes as he lowered his lips to hers. His mouth was infinitely tender as he kissed her. He made atonement for the violent kisses he had given her in what now seemed like another lifetime.

Laura angled her mouth beneath his and responded with considerably more passion than he'd expected. "Laura? Laura? Baby?" His lips pressed harder upon hers. His tongue sought the warmest depths of her mouth. She folded her arms across his back. Her legs shifted against his. She hugged his hips between her thighs.

"I'm getting hard again." He moaned.

"Are we going to do it again?"

"Can we?"

"Can't we?"

"You want to?" He looked down at her in amazement.

She nodded her head vigorously.

In an instant he left her and climbed off the bed. He undressed with reckless abandon, flinging away garments the moment he tore them off his body. Still lying on the bed, Laura undressed with the same kind of frenzy.

"What the hell am I doing?" James asked himself aloud. Standing naked beside the bed, he raked his hand through his hair and shook his head self-derisively.

His wife wet her lips. "I thought we were going to—"

"Oh, we are, baby, we are. But what's the rush?" Laura pointedly glanced down at his body, which gave every indication of urgency. He chuckled as he bent down and softly kissed her mouth. "It'll keep."

"Promise?"

"I promise," he said raspily. He lifted her onto the pillows and turned the covers back before he joined her on the bed.

Then, gently, he enfolded her in his arms. "You're beautiful. I like you naked." He kissed her mouth wantonly. His tongue was intimate. Timid at first, Laura soon gave herself up to the sensations that undulated through her as his lips explored her body.

Every part of her knew his sweet caresses, breasts and belly and thighs. Between them. He told her in husky whispers how much he loved tasting himself there.

And he continued tasting until she knew what he had apologized for moments earlier.

Even after that orgasmic initiation, she blushed at his bold touch and the audacious things he said. Not out of shame. Out of pure, undiluted joy. She was discovered, not degraded, by his caressing hands and mouth. Through his loving, she came to know herself.

And him. Never had she imagined that a man's body could be such a sensual feast. She thought he was beautiful. Once she had overcome an endearing shyness, she expressed her delight in him.

"Put your mouth there." He gently clasped her head between his hands and guided it to where her fingertips were curiously caressing. He sighed brokenly when she carried his instructions one step further and capriciously flicked her tongue against his skin. "Damn." He groaned. "I knew you'd be good. I knew it."

They spent the entire afternoon in bed, making love so many times and so frequently that the room became steamy. Their bodies grew slippery with sweat. Sunlight filtered in through the partially closed slats of the shutters and striped their nakedness with alluring shadows. Gradually those shadows lengthened and stretched across the walls and floor. Still they lay amidst the tangled, damp sheets, exploring, and exultant in their discoveries.

James suggested they cool off by taking a tepid bath. Laura sat between his thighs, her back resting on his chest, as he reclined against the tub. Lazily he ladled water over her breasts, watching as it trickled down her body and funneled between her thighs.

"I still can't believe I'm doing this with you," Laura said reflectively. Her hands were squeezing his thighs, testing the strength of the hard muscles beneath the hair-dusted skin.

"We're married."

"I can't believe that either," she said, laughing softly.

"Why?"

She shrugged, and he delighted in what the involuntary gesture did to her breasts. "I don't know. You're not at all what I thought I'd marry."

"You planned on marrying some milquetoast who wouldn't know how to begin to give you pleasure in bed."

She gave a clump of hair on his thigh a vicious tug, and he yelped. "Don't be so smug. What makes you so sure you're pleasuring me in bed?"

"I've got the battle scars to prove it." He cited a faint scratch on his shoulder.

"So I'm polite," she said with another of those shrugs he found so adorable.

"*Polite!*" His bellowing laughter echoed off the tile walls of the bathroom. "Baby, Emily Post never carried good manners *that* far."

"Shh!" she hissed. "And please spare me any boasts about your sexual expertise. They only remind me of how many lovers you've had. I never liked hearing about your conquests, even in high school."

He painted his initials on her bare shoulder with a wet fingertip. "I can understand how you would feel that way now. But why way back then?"

"I think I was jealous."

"Jealous?" Surprised, he sat up straighter, sloshing water onto the floor. "But you never even flirted with me."

"I wouldn't have dared. You were too dangerous to flirt with. I would have run in the opposite direction if you'd responded." She lowered her eyelids coyly. "That doesn't mean I wasn't intrigued. I'm intrigued by tigers, too, but I wouldn't want to be left alone with one."

"So I'm like a tiger, huh?" He slid his arms around her waist, pulled her higher against his lap, and made a snarling sound in her ear.

"Yes," she murmured, her eyes closing in pleasure. "Only hungrier. And wilder."

"And hornier."

He turned her around to face him. She complied. And by the time they got out to dry each other, there was more water on the floor than was left in the tub.

"Do you think we should put in an appearance at dinner?" Laura asked.

"Do we gotta?" He was holding her breasts in his palms, playfully aggravating her responsive nipples with his thumbs.

"I think we should, yes."

"Sure?"

He dropped to his knees.

"Hmm . . . uh . . . yes."

"Sure?"

She sighed his name.

* * *

Much later, dressed and walking arm in arm, they descended the staircase and entered the dining room. The table had been set with the finest china and silver. The crystal picked up the flickering light of the candles burning in the floral centerpiece.

"Mommy, Daddy," Mandy cried, sliding out of her chair when she saw them. She came running toward them and embraced them both around their legs. "I thought you'd never come downstairs! Gladys told me I had to sit nice and still and quiet until you did. She wouldn't let me go in your room and wake you up and she wouldn't give me anything to eat because she said it would spoil my dinner. I'm hungry. What took you so long? You sure did take a long nap."

"Sorry to keep you waiting, Tricks," James said without a trace of remorse. He scooped Mandy up with one arm, still keeping the other hooked through Laura's. "What's all this?" he asked, nodding toward the formally set dining-room table.

In answer, Gladys came bustling through the door that led into the kitchen. Heavenly smells wafted in behind her. "This is a special dinner, 'cause I think we all have something to celebrate." She gave the couple a broad, knowing smile.

"We certainly do," James said, surreptitiously sliding his arm down Laura's back and giving her bottom a light pinch.

"Sit down before dinner gets cold. I know you're hungry." The housekeeper's eyes rolled suggestively. When Laura blushed, she cackled with satisfaction.

The meal was sumptuous. It was one of the happiest occasions Laura could remember. She had thought she was in love with James before. But the love that welled up inside her now couldn't be contained. Frequently it sought an outlet in the form of tears. They caught the candlelight and glistened in her eyes every time she looked at him.

"Happy?" he asked, clasping her hand where it rested on the pristine tablecloth.

"Very."

"I'm getting there myself," he drawled teasingly. His eyes, partially closed and seductive, focused on her mouth.

Together they took Mandy upstairs to her room, where getting her undressed and into pajamas became a wrestling match. When she finally wound down, they saw that she was tucked into bed and listened to her prayers. She made supplications for everyone she knew and some she didn't know. When she began enumerating rock stars, James concluded the lengthy prayer with a firm "Amen," and turned off the lamp.

"Why so pensive?"

He came up behind Laura and placed his hands on her shoulders. She was sitting at her dressing table, staring vacantly into the mirror. As soon as they had returned to their suite, she had undressed and slipped into a silk wrapper. James had stripped down to his trousers.

"I was just thinking."

"About what?" he asked lightly.

"About . . ." She lowered her eyes demurely. "I'm not taking the pill or anything. And you didn't . . . uh . . ."

"Don't worry, I'll take care of it." He massaged her neck. "Preventing pregnancy isn't all that's on your mind, is it?"

"I have so many reasons to be happy." She

reached up and covered one of his hands with hers.

"Do I sense an unspoken 'but'?"

She smiled weakly. "It's just that I hesitate to bring up a subject that might spoil today."

His eyes met hers in the mirror. He withdrew his hands from her shoulders and wordlessly left the dressing room. Laura sighed, stood, and turned out the light. When she entered the bedroom, James was standing at the window, his hands shoved deep into his trouser pockets.

"You were right, James. It's none of my business."

He came around slowly. "Let me get one thing straight." She braced herself for his anger and was shocked when he said, "I wasn't angry at you this afternoon. I was mad at myself because you were so right."

She crossed the room quickly, took his hand, and led him to the bed, seating him on the fresh sheets Gladys had discreetly put on while they were having dinner. "I know it won't be easy for you, but try talking to me about it." Laura encouraged him by speaking softly and pressing his hands.

"There's nothing to talk about, really. I'm a real sonofabitch where my mother is concerned. I admit it. Beyond taking care of her material needs, I want nothing to do with her."

"Why?"

"Because she represents everything I was running away from when I left here over ten years ago. The poverty. The hand-to-mouth existence. The reputation of being the sorriest, poorest family in town."

"You rose above that."

"But she didn't!" He stood and began pacing. "I

begged her to leave with me, but she chose to stay with him."

"Him? Your father?"

"Father!" he said scornfully. "That drunken slob didn't know the meaning of the word." Pain, naked and bleak, filled his green eyes. "When I was a little kid I wanted to love him. I really did. I wanted to brag about my dad the way the other boys carried on about theirs.

"Then, when I realized what a no-account bum my father was, I felt ashamed. Other kids laughed at him, made fun of us. So I pretended that he wasn't my real father. I dreamed up an imaginary man who had been with my mother, just so I wouldn't have to admit being kin to the man who had actually fathered me."

Laura pressed her fingers against her lips to keep from making a sound, but tears filled her eyes. His pain touched her deeply. No wonder he had been such a hell-raiser. His rebellion had been a bid for attention, a substitute for the love lacking in his life. He had set out to prove that he was worthy of someone's notice.

"He used to beat us. Did you know that?" She made a gasping sound and shook her head. "Well, he did. I lived in constant fear of provoking him. Then, when I got big enough, I started fighting back. But that only made him madder, and when I wasn't there to protect her, he'd work Mother over."

Laura's shoulders slumped, and she covered her face with her hands. "Oh, God."

James spun around angrily. "Yeah, you can say that again. Where was *He*? Why does He let things like that happen to innocent people?"

"I don't know, James. I don't know." Tears

splashed against her face when she shook her head.

"I was determined to finish high school so I wouldn't be as ignorant as my old man. Then I worked in that stinking garage until I had saved enough money to split. But not before pleading with Mother to go too. She refused to leave him."

Even now he was bewildered by her decision, and shook his head in perplexity. "I couldn't understand why she would stay. But she did. When he died, I didn't even come back home for his funeral. I sent her money so she wouldn't be destitute, but I vowed never to feel sorry for her. She made her choice."

He flopped back down on the bed and hung his head in his hands, breathing heavily from anger and exertion. His dejection made him seem more touchable.

Laying a hand on his tousled hair, Laura selected her words carefully, then whispered, "Perhaps you're judging her too harshly, James. There could be many reasons why she didn't go with you."

"Like what? What would make a person stay with a violent, drunken fiend like that?"

"Fear of retribution, for one thing," she said. "Or love."

"Love?" he asked incredulously.

"Maybe. There's no explanation for love. Perhaps she loved him in spite of his violent temper. Or maybe she was too proud to leave him. I understand that it's very difficult for a woman to admit that her husband values her so little as to physically abuse her."

Laura lovingly touched his face. "Or maybe she stayed to protect you, James. I'm sure she wanted you to have a better life than she did. She could have been afraid he'd come after you both if she didn't stay behind. I think she made a tremendous sacrifice for you. Even to the point of risking her life."

Laura could see the ambivalence in his features as he studied his hands, turning them this way and that while deep in thought. She sensed that he was viewing Leona's decision in a whole new light. His previous convictions weren't so steadfast now.

"James," she asked quietly, "are you ashamed of your mother? Are you afraid that an association with her will remind people of where you came from? Is that why you don't want to see or be seen with her?"

He said nothing for a moment, then turned his head. "Whew! You fight dirty, don't you? You hit below the belt." He left the bed again and prowled the room aimlessly. "If that were true, I'd be a real bastard, wouldn't I?" He expected no answer and got none. "But I guess that's been in the back of my mind." Sighing, he dragged his hand down his face. "What kind of person does that make me, Laura?"

"Human." She extended her hand to him. He took it gratefully and let her pull him down to lie beside her. She cradled his head between her breasts, smoothing her hand over his hair.

"Your mother is a real lady, James. I like her very much."

"You do?"

"Yes. She's gracious and kind. Eager to please."

"Does she really have a picture of me?"

"In a silver frame. Displayed in the most promi- nent place in her house."

"It must be the only picture ever taken of me before I left home." A trace of the old bitterness was in his voice.

"That's probably why she values it so much." Her calm rejoinder quelled his resurgence of hostility.

"I guess it wouldn't hurt to call her."

Because he couldn't see her face, Laura clamped her lower lip between her teeth and squeezed her eyes shut in profound relief. After a moment she said, "She won't make the first move toward a reconciliation. She respects you too much. I think she's in awe of you."

"I don't know, Laura," he said skeptically. "It's been a decade. There's been a lot of water under the bridge. I'm probably not what she wants or needs, not even what she expects."

"Have no doubts on that score. You're her son. Her baby. She loves you and would forgive you anything. I'm sure the inadequacies you feel can't compare to her feelings of inferiority."

For a long time, Laura continued to hold him, giving him the maternal cosseting he'd been deprived of as a boy. Leona Paden had loved her son. But survival, hers and James's, had been a daily challenge. She hadn't had the luxury of nurturing him spiritually.

At thirty-three, he sought that nurturing in the arms of his loving wife. Laura ran her fingers through his hair and idly scratched his back, whispering endearments. She was certain that he would mend his relationship with his mother, but something else disturbed her.

"James?"

"Hmm?"

"Are you still angry at God?"

After a time, he said, "He made it all up to me and we came to terms."

"How?"

Very simply he said, "He gave me Mandy."

He almost added, "And you." But he didn't. And in a short while they both fell asleep.

He had already gone downstairs when Laura awakened the following morning. Wearing a smile that simply wouldn't go away, she showered and dressed quickly and joined him and Mandy in the breakfast room. Mandy was giggling.

"What's so funny?" Laura asked from the doorway.

James swung around to look at her, and her heart soared at the impact his glowing eyes had on her. She recalled all the times he had reached for her during the night. There had been a childlike desperation in his touch, as though she might vanish if he lost physical contact with her. She'd been there, ready with a reassuring word, a soft caress, a kiss.

"Daddy's tickling me. Do it to Mommy, do it to Mommy," Mandy chanted, hopping up and down in her chair.

"Only too happy to oblige." James left his place at the table and moved toward Laura. For Mandy's benefit, he slid his hands up and down her rib cage as though he were tickling her. For his benefit, he kissed her accommodating mouth. His lips slid beneath her hair to her ear. "Too bad I can't tickle you like I did yesterday. I really made you squirm. Remember?"

Laura blushed to the roots of her hair. He laughed, pleased in a possessive, masculine way. After another hard, swift kiss, he escorted her to the table. As soon as they'd eaten breakfast, he excused himself, saying that he had errands to run. Laura told Mandy to help Gladys carry the dishes to the sink and followed him out. She reached the entrance hall just as he was shrugging into his sports jacket.

"Going anyplace in particular?" she asked with affected nonchalance.

He gave her a crooked smile and took a square, cream-colored envelope from his breast pocket. She recognized it as one of the party invitations. Leona Paden's name was scrawled across it.

"Don't you need a stamp?"

"This one gets hand-delivered."

"Oh, James, I—" She almost told him then that she loved him. Catching the spontaneous words just in time, she satisfied herself by stepping into the circle of his arms and returning his hearty hug. "Would you like me to go with you?"

"Yes," he confessed, clenching her tighter. But he shook his head and pushed her away. "I would love to have you there to lend moral support. But this is something I've got to do alone." There was no humor behind his short laugh. "I'm more nervous about meeting my own mother face-to-face than I ever was before a car race."

She ran her hands over his lapels. "She'll be much more nervous than you."

He cocked his head to one side and squinted down at his wife. "You know, for a sexy broad, you've got a lot of human kindness."

"Why, Mr. Paden," she simpered, southern-belle style, "I do declare! I never knew you had such a winnin' way with words."

He laughed in appreciation of her posturing, but then turned serious. "Thank you, Laura, for making me do this."

She shook her head in denial. "You would have done it by yourself sooner or later. I only gave you a boost."

"Still . . ."

He had every intention of giving her a tender, husbandly kiss of gratitude. But his arms wrapped around her malleable body, and the kiss lengthened and grew hotter until his manhood responded. He set her away from him. "Later, baby."

Before he submitted to his impulses, he stalked out the front door, letting the screen slap closed behind him.

The next few days were devoted to preparations for the party. The guest list was continuously updated, and invitations were rushed to the post office in time to go out in the afternoon mail.

"Why didn't we just put an ad in the paper and issue a blanket invitation to everybody in town?" James asked dryly as Laura thrust another batch of stamped envelopes into his hand to be mailed. "Just kidding," he said when she looked up at him, horrified by the suggestion.

Over Gladys's strenuous protests, Laura hired a caterer to help with the food for the party. The caterer and the housekeeper had battles royal, but finally agreed on a menu. It was to be a typically southern spread, with steamed crab and prawns, battered fried fish, fried chicken, corn on the cob, baked beans, okra gumbo, along with salads and relishes and watermelon and Gladys's famous pecan tarts for dessert.

James hired a crew of boys still out of school for summer vacation to help Bo manicure the vast lawns surrounding the house. The lower branches of the trees were lined with tiny clear Christmas lights to give the whole yard a fairyland aura, which delighted Mandy. Lanterns were strung along invisible wires that ran from tree to tree, and the pier was lined with torches planted in buckets of sand. A dance band from Atlanta would provide the music.

"Only one thing bothers me," Laura mused aloud late one afternoon. They were walking their horses back to the stables after taking a ride with Mandy.

"What's that?" James swung down from his mount to assist Laura off hers. Bo had already assisted Mandy. "What could go wrong? Laura, the White House staff doesn't go to this much trouble to plan a state dinner for the visiting premier of China. What stone could you have possibly left unturned?"

"The weather." Worriedly, she glanced up at the sky. "There's a storm brewing down in the Caribbean, and the weathermen are saying that by the weekend we might get rain." She gnawed at her lower lip. "That would spoil everything."

"I don't think so." James grabbed her around the waist and lifted her off her feet. "We could send everybody home early and have our own party in the privacy of our bedroom." He nuzzled the V of her open collar, which was on a level with his nose. "Just the two of us. Nekkid and nasty. BYOBO."

"BYOBO?"

"Bring your own baby oil." She smiled, but the worried frown between her brows didn't fade. "Look, baby," James said with a long-suffering sigh, "it's not going to rain. Okay? *Okay?*" he repeated, shaking her slightly until she agreed with him.

"Okay," she mumbled. He imitated her pout. Only, he did it much better. He looked adorable. "Okay!" She finally succumbed to laughter.

*   *   *

The day before the party, around noon, James descended the dim steps leading to the cellar. "Yoo-hoo!"

"Down here."

"I know, but where?" he asked, reaching the bottom.

"Over here. Gladys sent me down to take last-minute inventory. She's making the final, final, *final* run to the grocery store today." Laura was standing in front of a storage shelf, making additions to a growing list. "What are you doing home? I thought you had business in town. Is it lunch-time already?" Surveying her list, she absently tapped her pencil against her cheek. "Did you see Leona? I asked her over to help Gladys arrange flowers."

"Yes, I had business in town, but I finished it earlier than I thought I would." James caught his wife around the waist and turned her about to face him. He took the notebook and pencil out of her astonished hands and tossed them down on a worktable that an ancestor had fortuitously provided.

"Yes, it's lunchtime already. Yes, I saw Mother and Gladys and Tricks out on the terrace arranging flowers. In fact they told me where I might find you, and now that I have your attention, Mrs. Paden, how about giving your husband a hello kiss?"

Before she could answer, he sealed his mouth over hers, parted her surprised lips even wider, and swept her mouth with his tongue. "There," he murmured several heart-stopping moments later, "that's more like the welcome I had in mind."

"Any time," Laura said breathlessly.

"Really?" One corner of his lip tilted into a sexy smile. "I can't tell you how glad I am to hear you say that, darlin', because I have a real hankering for you right now."

"Right now?"

He moved forward, backing her against the edge of the table. "Uh-huh. I want a taste." He reached for the buttons of her blouse and had them undone before Laura knew what had happened. Beneath her blouse he found a frilly pastel teddy and muttered his appreciation.

"I wanted to see your undies."

"What? When?" His hands were moving over her breasts, making her almost incoherent.

"Always. When I'd see you walking down the sidewalks of town and in the halls at school. I was dying to know what kind of undies rich girls wore. What kind Laura Nolan wore. I'd have gone crazy for sure if I'd ever imagined anything like this." He peeled the lacy cups down over her breasts and bent his head to take the tip of one between his lips.

She clutched at his hair for balance. "James," she whimpered as his tongue laved her beguilingly.

"You're delicious." His lips closed around the pouting flesh and sucked gently.

She moaned. "Someone might . . ." Her eyes flickered toward the top of the steps, where light from the open cellar door poured in. But it barely registered on her whirling mind before her eyes closed of their own accord.

His hands moved up her thighs beneath her full, casual skirt. They caressed their way up to her waist and lifted her onto the table. He stepped between her thighs.

"Look what you do to me." He pressed her hand to the front of his trousers.

"It's the middle of the day." No protest had ever sounded so feeble.

He rubbed himself against her palm. "I've been this way since morning."

"Even after last night?"

"Every time I see you, think about you."

She gave a short, startled cry when he unsnapped the teddy and caressed her where she was already wet and warm. The sound of his zipper could barely be heard over the rapid soughing of their breathing.

"Always so sweet and small."

That was his last strangled groan. After that, their words weren't discernible.

Several minutes later, he eased himself off her and helped her up to perch on the edge of the table. "How do you feel about the cellar now?" he asked gently, running a finger down her cheek.

"Well, if that didn't banish my fears, nothing will." She gave him a bashful smile so out of keeping with her lustiness only moments earlier that he grinned.

Considerately he passed her a handkerchief. When she was finished with it, she stuffed it in her skirt pocket and restored her clothing. Between kisses, James helped her. It was he who closed the last button on her blouse, and he did so only after stealing one last glimpse of her breasts.

"James, you didn't use—"

"I keep forgetting to go to the drugstore."

"You know the risk we're taking."

"Do you really want to talk about that now?" He eased her off the table. Her knees were weak, she discovered when she tried to stand. Slumping against him, she curled her arms around his neck for support and rested her cheek against his chest. "No, I guess not."

He rubbed her back soothingly. "What would you like to talk about?"

"About how decadent I've become." A chuckle rumbled up from his chest. "Isn't there a law against corrupting the morals of a very nice lady?"

"I don't think you were really all that nice," he whispered directly into her ear. "I think you were a decadent wanton hiding behind a disguise of primness and propriety. You were ripe for a mean stud like me to come along and sweep you off your feet."

She sighed with resignation. "I suppose so. Otherwise I couldn't have been corrupted so easily."

"You *were* a pushover."

Rather than take offense, she merely smiled, drinking in his familiar scent. "Is it true what they say, that a man wants his wife to be a lady in the parlor and a whore in the bedroom?"

"Where do you come up with all this stuff?" He angled his head back to glance down at her.

"*Is* it?"

"I guess that comes close to summing it up."

"Remember the other night, when you turned the air-conditioner down low and built a fire in the fireplace?"

"Yeah? So?"

"I've become a whore in the parlor too."

Her face and inflection were so anxiety-ridden that he burst into laughter. Hugging her hard, he rocked her back and forth. "You're some woman, Miss Laura. Dear heaven, you make me feel good."

He kissed her again with feeling, then left his lips against hers to say, "I've got a question for you, baby."

"What?" she asked expectantly.

He smiled that slow, arrogant smile she had come to know and love so well. "What's for lunch?"

Nine

The day of the party dawned gray and overcast. The low pressure system Laura had expressed concern about had been officially upgraded to a tropical storm, with winds in excess of fifty miles an hour circulating around its nucleus.

"I'm sure it won't bother us," James assured her when she mentioned it again after watching the weather reports on television. "It's still miles off-shore. Even if it moves toward the coast, it will probably have blown itself out by the time it reaches us. This is the first storm of the season, and that rarely amounts to much."

Laura pushed her worry into the back of her mind and forced herself into a party mood. The atmosphere was muggy, but, as the day progressed, the humidity seemed to lighten along with her mood. By late afternoon 22 Indigo Place had taken on a festive air.

Mandy was almost too excited. Like a frisky puppy, she was underfoot and in the way and driving everyone to distraction.

"Mother, could you please entertain Mandy so Laura and I can dress?" James asked Leona when she arrived, wearing a dress he had bought her for the occasion.

She had had her hair and nails done at the beauty shop. She was long past vanity, but knew that this evening was important to James and didn't want him to be ashamed of her. The worry lines that had been engraved on her face years ago were relieved now by smiles. She looked unusually pretty.

Leona had been a frequent visitor to the house since the reconciliation with her son. Laura hadn't asked James for the details of their reunion, but when he returned home that day, he had held her for a long moment before saying, "You were right. My mother is quite a lady."

Now Leona Paden smiled up at him fondly and took her granddaughter's hand. "Don't worry about Mandy and me. We'll take care of each other, won't we, Mandy?"

"Sure, Grandma! Let's go get Annmarie dressed for the party."

Leona led the child away, and James dashed upstairs to finish dressing.

"How do I look?" he asked Laura anxiously as he preened in front of the mirror. "Should I wear something else?"

"You look casually elegant. In a word, perfect." He was dressed in moss-green linen slacks, a shirt of the same color, but in a softer weave, and a cream-colored linen sport coat. The woodsy colors complemented his eyes and hair. He had never looked more handsome.

Laura draped her arms around his neck and kissed him softly. "Don't worry, James. Everyone will be suitably impressed. And if they're not, who cares? They don't matter." But she knew that it mattered a great deal to him what people thought. After all, that had been the original reason for having the party.

"I don't want to look like scum playing dress-up."

Her heart swelled to overflowing with love for him. She ached for every time he'd been slighted. Holding his face between her hands, she whispered, "You look exactly like what you are, a successful businessman, a country gentleman who has a lovely home, a father whose daughter worships him, and a husband whose wife . . ."

"Don't stop there. A wife who what?"

Who loves you with all my heart, she wanted to say. Instead she coquettishly cocked her head to one side and said, "Who wouldn't mind being on the receiving end of a compliment, even an insincere one."

He subjected her to a leisurely inspection. Her dress was a vivid purple, a color that didn't flatter most women. But the vibrant color intensified the blue of her eyes, the rosy bloom in her cheeks, and the sunlit gold of her hair. The sleeveless dress had a ruffled neckline that cut straight across her collarbone, but was scooped out all the way to her waist in back. The full skirt swirled around her calves, almost touching the ankle straps of her white sandals. Her hair was piled on top of her head and secured there with white camellias.

"You look ravishing. And I'm giving some serious thought to ravishing you. And if you doubt my sincerity, well . . ." He grasped her hips and pulled her forward, positioning his body against hers. *"That's* sincere."

His mouth was open and warm as it lazily moved over hers, sipping, touching her lips lightly with the tip of his tongue. His hands flattened on her bare back and stroked the smooth skin. Then one ventured to her breast and fondled it.

"Hmm, James, stop," she said, gasping, and tore her mouth free. "We can't."

He released her without a struggle. "As I've told you before, it'll keep."

His wink was suggestive, his expression seductive, and there was no doubt in Laura's mind how they would celebrate after the party was over. She couldn't wait.

All James's anxiety had been for naught. He wasn't only accepted, he was kowtowed to by everyone he met or with whom he renewed acquaintanceship. People clustered around him. It was an effort for him to get around to speak to everyone during the course of the evening.

Often Laura linked her arm through his with a surge of possessive jealousy when female guests became a little too effusive in welcoming him back to town. She was always gratified when James covered her hand with his own and pressed it warmly. No matter how attractive and determined a woman was to win his notice, his wife could always distract his attention.

If only he had told her he loved her, just once, Laura would have considered herself the luckiest woman alive. But not even during their most impassioned lovemaking had he ever said those three simple words.

Gazing up at his profile as he shook hands with Gregory's mayor and set a golf date, Laura knew that what she had was enough. She had given him the respectability he sought. His gratitude was hers, if not his love. That was sufficient.

He proudly introduced both his mother and his daughter to their guests. Hardly anyone in town could associate the bedraggled widow of the town drunk with the quiet, gracious woman who basked in her son's success and her granddaughter's affection.

The guests gorged themselves on gossip about their host and hostess and the apparent regard they held for each other. They consumed the food, the drink, and the scenery that 22 Indigo Place had always been famous for.

It was close to midnight before the last of them wandered down the lane toward their parked cars, murmuring among themselves that the party had been the best of the summer season and that it would be a long time before the Padens were outdone.

"Ah, that feels good," Laura said, easing off her sandals. She had been on her feet for hours. Sitting at the kitchen table, she worked the circulation back into her toes.

"Here, baby, dig in." James set a plate heaped with food in front of her. "I didn't see you take a bite all night." He had filled a plate for himself as well, and they fell to eating hungrily. "Mother, you're spending the night here, aren't you?" he asked Leona between mouthfuls.

"If you want me to."

"I do. Gladys has already fixed up the spare bedroom for you. Why don't you and Mandy go on upstairs? You both look exhausted."

Mandy sleepily made her rounds, giving everyone a good-night kiss before she let her grandmother lead her upstairs to bed. Gladys fussed over James and Laura, admonishing them for not eating at their own party. As she went about cleaning up the party debris in the kitchen, she kept their plates filled.

The back screen door squeaked when Bo came in, having seen to it that all the lanterns and torches were safely extinguished and that the grounds were secure for the night. He looked worried. "Laura, James, I just heard on the radio that the storm has been upgraded to a hurricane."

Suddenly losing her appetite, Laura pushed her plate aside. She spoke her husband's name, her voice sounding desperate.

"Turn on the TV." Gladys reached for the dials of the portable set she kept in the kitchen so she could watch her favorite soap operas in the afternoons as she worked.

Betty, as the storm had been named, was the major story on the late-night news shows. It had been a full-scale hurricane for several hours. Winds of over a hundred miles an hour were reported by the Navy. Even on the satellite photographs the storm looked fearsome and potentially devastating. The coasts of Georgia and the Carolinas lay in its current path.

"Indigo Place." Laura, her face pale, her voice faint with terror, turned to James. "What should we do?"

"There's nothing we can do tonight except get a good night's sleep," he said, taking her in his arms. He patted her back as his lips moved through her hair. "And in the morning, we'll reassess the situation. These storms can change course in a matter of hours."

The Burtons went to their quarters behind the main house, their shoulders stooped with worry. James tried to lead Laura from the kitchen, but she dug in her heels. "No, you go ahead. I'm not sleepy."

"You are not going to stay down here with your ear glued to a radio, Laura."

"Why not? I'm worried."

"So am I, but what good is it going to do to sit

here and chart that storm? There's nothing we can do."

She clamped her lower lip between her teeth and wrung her hands. "I can't just go upstairs to bed as if this were any other night. It's like turning my back on Indigo Place. Deserting it."

He looked at her as though she were a recalcitrant child and gently took her shoulders between his hands. "What good will you be to Indigo Place if you exhaust yourself? Come on, now. No more arguments."

She went reluctantly, but docilely. By the time he closed the door of the bedroom, she had relinquished her willpower to him and moved like one entranced. Her arms hung heavily at her sides. Since she was incapable of undressing herself, he did it for her. When he had removed her clothing, he took his off quickly and led her to bed. Beneath the covers, Laura shivered, though it was warm.

His arms went around her and pulled her against him so tightly that there was no space between them. Then he loved her. And it had nothing to do with sex.

Sifting his fingers through her hair, which his own hands had let down, he whispered to her in the dark, comforting, soothing words, until she stopped trembling.

His lips lay close to her temple and frequently he kissed it lightly, telling her how much he appreciated the party she had given in his honor and what a success he thought it had been. Finally, with her face nestling against his furry chest, she drifted to sleep.

The news the following morning was grim.
Side by side, Laura and James sat on the leather

sofa in her father's study and watched television. All programming had been preempted in favor of news bulletins regarding hurricane Betty.

Forgotten were the assurances James had whispered to her last night. Laura was disconsolate at the thought of life without 22 Indigo Place, because that would also mean life without James. The destruction of the house would be tantamount to the destruction of her marriage. The marriage had been founded upon the house. No house, no marriage.

Gladys kept hot coffee in constant supply, though neither of them wanted anything to eat or drink. Leona was asked to stay and help occupy Mandy. The child couldn't play outside because it had started to rain. Inside the gloomy house, she was bored and thereby contrary, adding to the strain on everyone's nerves.

Civil defense authorities urged people to evacuate the area when it seemed certain that the Georgia coast would be the most likely place the storm would move ashore. St. Gregory's Sound was already churning with turbulence.

"I won't leave," Laura said, stubbornly shaking her head. "I'll never leave Indigo Place."

James's mouth twisted in irritation at her irrationality, but he said nothing. He pulled on tall rubber fishing boots and a slicker and braved the elements outside. The plywood he and Bo nailed over the windows of the house wouldn't keep out the storm, but James felt that he had to do something or go crazy. He couldn't just sit around as though he were keeping vigil at a deathbed. He hated not being in control. It was frustrating that a storm had the upper hand.

Even though the exodus from the coastal towns had begun and traffic was snarled on all the highways leading west, James managed to get several horse trailers through. Forlornly Laura watched from the front porch as the skittish horses were led through torrential rains into the trailers and driven away.

Her despair was as thick as the atmosphere. It took a supreme effort to draw the heavy air into her chest, which was constricted with emotion.

"Will you help pack Mandy a bag? Mother might miss something she needs."

James had found his wife sitting alone in the parlor. All the windows had been covered and the atmosphere was funereal. He didn't think Laura had heard him, and he was about to repeat his request when she turned around and looked at him with vacant eyes.

"Pack?"

"I'm sending Mandy and Mother with the Burtons. I got through on the telephone and found a motel in Macon that isn't full yet. I made a reservation for them, but if they're not there by the specified time, the room will be given to someone else."

She nodded vaguely and went upstairs to help Leona gather Mandy's things into a suitcase. When they were ready to leave, Laura crouched down to kiss Mandy good-bye."

"I'm not scared, but Annmarie is," the child said through quivering lips. "I told her not to be afraid."

"You're both very brave." Laura ran both hands over Mandy's head.

"I don't want to leave you and Daddy, but he said you'd take care of each other. Will you?"

"Of course."

"You won't be scared?"

"No. We won't be scared."

"I love you, Mommy."

Laura clutched the warm, vital, child's body against hers, actually drawing strength from it, wishing she could be imbued with Mandy's faith. "I love you, too, darling. Be sweet for Grandma and Gladys and Bo."

"Come on, Tricks," James said gently, breaking them apart. "You don't want the motel man to give your room away to someone else, do you?"

Mandy's lips were trembling uncontrollably as Bo carried her to the car through the pelting rain and handed her into the back seat and Leona's waiting arms. Pathetically she gazed out the rear window and waved at James and Laura until the car rounded the bend and drove out of sight.

Laura's heart was wrenching, but she knew she was experiencing just a taste of the hurt she would feel if James and Mandy left her life forever.

"I wish you'd reconsider, Laura. We ought to be following them to Macon."

Her jaw was set as she looked up at him stubbornly and shook her head. However, the choice was taken away from her several hours later when a deputy sheriff pounded on the front door.

All afternoon the rain had continued to beat down. The wind had increased in velocity. The storm gave no evidence of abating. In fact, the weather experts keeping an eye on Betty predicted that it would be one of the worst hurricanes of recent history.

"Sorry, Mr. Paden," the deputy shouted over the howling winds. Rainwater dripped from the wide brim of his hat. He was covered from chin to ankles in a yellow slicker. "Looks like we're gonna bear the brunt of this one. Everybody's got to get out. You have half an hour before I come back."

"We'll be gone," James grimly promised.

Closing the door, he turned to face Laura, who

was standing behind him in the entrance hall. "Do you want to take anything with you?"

She was willing to sacrifice her life, not for the salvation of 22 Indigo Place, but for the salvation of her marriage. Time! Why hadn't she been granted more time? If only she'd had another day, a week, a month, she might have made James love her. As it was, she was being forced to throw in the towel before the last bell. The fight was over.

The starch went out of her and her whole body sagged with defeat. "No, I don't want to take anything with me."

Nothing tangible had value anymore. God, what a fool she'd been to place so much value on things. Property. Lineage. From the cradle she'd been taught to treasure all that, but she should have been wise enough to figure out long ago that people were so much more valuable than things. Than pride. Than reputation.

That was why she had never married, never really loved. She'd never given anyone priority over a piece of ground and a house. Until James. She was learning the lesson the hard way, by having to sacrifice the one she loved most dearly.

They took only the time necessary to collect toilet articles and put a change of underwear into an overnight bag. James brought the car around and pulled it up near the porch. Laura closed the front door of the house and laid her palm against the cool wood. It was like placing her hand on the heart of a loved one, fearing that at any moment it was going to stop beating.

At last, sniffing back her tears, she turned and ran down the steps to the car.

Glass crunched under James's boot heels. "It's

worse than I thought," he said, bending down to pick up a piece of the priceless chandelier that had once hung over the dining-room table.

He looked angry. He hurled the piece of crystal down, and it shattered on the pile of debris at his feet. Laura, watching him, swallowed her despair and turned away.

The previous forty-eight hours had been a nightmare. The drive to Macon had been one of the most nerve-wracking experiences of her life. The bumper-to-bumper traffic had been further impeded by the rain. Frightened people just like her had been fleeing their homes, wondering if they would have a home to return to after Betty took her toll.

They had found the others already safely tucked into the small motel room. There wasn't another vacant room in Macon. Chivalrously James and Bo had offered to sleep in the cars, leaving the room to the ladies. Laura got very little sleep that first night. Mandy, who had shared her bed, kicked like a young colt; Gladys snored; Leona made moaning sounds. But worry was mostly responsible for keeping Laura's eyes open.

Her worst fears were realized the following morning when the newspapers and television reported that Gregory had been hit hard by the hurricane. The very eye of the storm had passed over the town, so it had sustained the whiplashing winds and rain twice. Several tornadoes had been spawned and had left swaths of destruction in their wakes. Through the endless day, they monitored the newscasts.

Not for another twenty-four hours, until the floodwaters had receded and it was deemed safe, were they permitted to return to Gregory. James had decided to leave the others in Macon. So that they would be more comfortable, he got another motel room as soon as one became available.

"Until I know what the situation is at home, you're better off here," he had told the dejected group. "We'll be in touch as soon as we know something." Before he and Laura left for Gregory, he pressed money into Bo's hand, kissed his mother and Mandy, and commissioned Gladys to take care of them.

Their return trip had been essentially silent. Speculating on how much damage Indigo Place might have sustained was pointless. As they neared the coast, signs of devastation had prepared them for the worst.

Laura's heart had leaped with gladness when they drove through the gate and she saw that the exterior walls of the house were still standing. Of course there was an ugly line on the white painted brick that marked how high the muddy floodwaters had risen. A portion of the roof had been blown off and the windows broken out, but the structure was still there.

But now James's mumbled curses did little to revive her flagging spirits. As he surveyed the storm damage, he was no doubt thinking that he had made a bad investment. He had gambled a small fortune on Indigo Place and it hadn't paid off. It would take another small fortune to have the house cleaned and repaired, not even taking into account the heirloom furnishings that would have to be replaced. Insurance would cover some, but not all, of the loss.

And, realistically, why should he bother? Why go to all that trouble and expense now that it was no longer necessary? He had achieved his goal. The town that had scorned him was lying in the palm of his hand. He had accomplished what he had set out to do. He had proved himself worthy of its respect. If he were going to sink a fortune into a house, it could be in Atlanta or anywhere else in the world. It no longer had to be in Gregory.

When he left, would he offer to take her with him? Laura wondered. That was the question uppermost in her mind. She had served her purpose. He had married her for her name and her address. He didn't need them any longer, and they wouldn't amount to a hill of beans outside Gregory County. What they shared in bed he could find anywhere with countless other women.

"I'm going to check the stables." She hurried away before he could see the tears welling in her eyes or hear the giveaway gruffness in her voice.

She waded through the sea of mud, heedless of her boots and the hem of her jeans. It broke her heart to see one of the main branches of a live oak severed from the majestic trunk that had withstood storms for over a century. The pier James had put so many hours into repairing was gone. But that didn't hurt nearly as much as the heartache of having to give up James and Mandy.

Twenty-two Indigo Place was destructible. Testimony to its impermanence lay everywhere she looked. But her love for James would never die. Indigo Place was her past. He was her future.

She entered the shadowed stables, which, miraculously, had been left intact. Water had flooded the huge barn, but she climbed the ladder to the hayloft, which was still dry and fragrant. She lay down on an old blanket, curled her body into a tight, protective ball, and wept.

"Laura?"

She didn't know how long she had been crying, but sat bolt upright at the sound of James's voice.

She wiped her tear-streaked face with the backs of her hands. "Up here," she called down.

A weak, late-afternoon sun was seeping through the shingled roof. Dust motes danced in the faint golden light. The stables smelled musty and damp, but not unpleasantly so.

"I couldn't find you anywhere," James eased himself up through the trap door.

"I used to come here often when I needed to be alone to think."

"Or to cry," he said bluntly, dropping down beside her.

She lowered her eyes. "Aren't I entitled to? Just a little?"

"I guess so."

He sounded distant, hostile, and Laura held her silence. When she could bear the tension no longer, she asked, "What are your plans?"

He draped his arms loosely over his raised knees. He was chewing on a straw, and moved it from one corner of his lips to the other. "I guess we'll start with the roof to make the house weather-tight again. I think we'll need a cleaning crew to come in—What's the matter?" He had noticed her expression. Her face was blank with surprise.

"You—you're going to restore Indigo Place?"

"Hell, yes. What else? Do you think we could live in it the way it is?"

She swallowed quickly. "Then you plan to go on living here?"

"We'll have to rent something in town until the reconstruction is finished." He was using plural pronouns. Laura's heart began to pound with hope. Again he noticed her stunned expression, and took immediate offense. "What's the matter? Don't you trust me to do the reconstruction right? Afraid I'll mess up your family's estate?"

Tears shone in her eyes. She shook her head. "No. It's not that. I didn't think you'd do the reconstruction at all."

He studied her for a moment. "Care to explain why you would think such a thing?"

"Indigo Place was the reason you married me. Now that it's gone and you don't need me anymore—"

She never got to finish. He yanked hard on her arm and pulled her across his lap, until she was reclining on his thighs and his face was close to hers as he bent over her. "Don't need you anymore? Baby, I need you in a way I didn't think it was possible to need anybody, especially a woman."

He bracketed her jaw with one strong hand, tilted her head back, and ground a rapacious kiss onto her mouth. They hadn't touched each other since the night of the party and they were slightly crazed from sexual deprivation. Laura's body immediately wilted from the heat of his. She greedily returned his kiss and clasped his head between her hands.

When they finally fell apart, they were breathless. "What do you mean, I don't need you?" he demanded. "Can't you feel it? Can't you see it in my eyes every time I look at you? I stay hungry for you."

"You wanted my name, my position in the community."

"At first, yes. I came to town with every intention of buying Indigo Place and wooing you into marriage for exactly the reason you said. But I don't care now if you picked cotton for a living. I want you." He held her head pressed between his hands, almost hurtfully, and delved into her eyes with his.

"Why were you crying all afternoon? Because you thought you had lost Indigo Place?"

He allowed her enough leverage to shake her head. "Because I thought that losing it would mean losing you. You are what I couldn't bear to part with. The house is dispensable. You're not."

He seared the walls of the loft with swear words. They could have passed as prayers. "There was no chance in hell of your losing me, Miss Laura." He lowered his head to her breasts and pressed hot, damp kisses through her blouse. "Why do you think I've been trying my damnedest to get you pregnant? Baby, I've been hoping that I'd make a baby in you. I wanted a guarantee that you wouldn't walk out on me."

She moaned beneath the sweet assault of his mouth and returned his kisses with a fervor he had taught her. "Then why have you been acting so angry? I was afraid you considered Indigo Place and me a bad investment."

"No, no." He rubbed the words into her neck with his lips. "I was angry because you were so upset over the storm and worried about the house. I wanted you to care more for Mandy and me than you did for it."

"Oh, James, I do! Didn't you realize that?" She pulled on his hair until he raised his head. "I'm a fool for not telling you something I've known for a long time." She hesitated.

"Well?"

"I love you."

He grew very still. "You do?"

"I was always infatuated with you. Even before that night you rescued me from those boys and brought me home on your motorcycle. You attracted me because I knew you were something I could never have. Then, when you came back to town . . . well, it started all over again. You made me restless, and I thought it was just that infatuation starting all over again. But weeks ago I realized that the infatuation had turned into love."

He brushed the loose strands of hair away from her face. "I love you, too, Laura. I'm rotten to the core. No sense in pretending otherwise. And you're such a lady, an aristocrat. I thought you'd scoff at me if I told you how I feel about you, so I didn't risk it. But I'm telling you now. I love you."

She touched his face, loving the brooding sulkiness of his mouth, the insolence in his eyes, loving most his vulnerability. He had revealed this susceptible part of himself only to her, and that was a true testament of his love. "You're not nearly the bad boy you pretend to be, James Paden."

"Keep my secret?"

"Promise."

Stillness surrounded them as they slowly began to remove their clothes. The sun was setting. The shadows in the loft were penetrating, though a few fiery rays burned through the cracks in the shingles overhead like tiny spotlights. The stable was redolent with the smell of hay and earth, rain and flesh.

Naked, they knelt on the blanket facing each other, touching only with their lips. Then his hands covered her breasts and massaged them lovingly.

"Have my baby?"

"Yes, yes."

"When it comes, can I taste your milk?"

He lowered his head. His breath was soft, but rapid. His mouth was gentle, but erotic.

Sighing with pleasure, she separated her knees. "Touch me."

He did, pressing his open hand over her mound,

then sliding it between her thighs. His thumb was breathtakingly knowledgeable.

She reached for him. Beneath her questing fingers he was hard and smooth and warm and already brimming with passion.

They caressed each other into a glorious frenzy.

Seconds before the tumult came, he lifted her astride his lap and impaled her.

Much later, their bodies were dewy with perspiration as they lay facing each other, replete and languid. "I love you," she whispered, tracing his sullen lower lip with her fingernail.

"I love you."

She kissed him, a dry, quick, fleeting kiss, and moved to get up.

He caught her wrist. "Where do you think you're going?"

Hay was clinging to the tangles in her hair. Her mouth had been rouged by his ardent kisses. She looked at him with china-blue eyes belonging to a woman thoroughly besotted with her lover. Her whole body was rosy with the aftermath of satisfying lovemaking.

"I—I thought we'd dress and go into town . . . find a place to spend the night . . . look for . . ."

Her voice trailed off. The corner of his mouth was curving into a suggestive smile. He looked up at her with drowsy, heavy-lidded eyes. His sultry expression could have talked an angel out of her wings. And more.

"No way, baby. I just discovered that I do some of my best work in the hay."

Then, hooking his hand around the back of her neck, he pulled her down again.

THE EDITOR'S CORNER

Do you grumble as much as I do about there being too few hours in the day? Time. There just never seems to be enough of it! That seemed especially to be the case a few weeks ago when we were sitting here facing a scheduling board with every slot filled for months and months . . . and an embarrassment of goodies (finished LOVESWEPT manuscripts, of course). But, then, suddenly, it occurred to us that the real world limitations of days and months didn't necessarily apply to a publishing schedule. Voilà! 1986 got rearranged a bit as we created a thirteenth month in the year for a unique LOVESWEPT publishing event. Our thirteenth month features three special romances going on sale October 15, 1986.

What's so remarkable that it warrants the creation of a month? Another "first" in series romance from LOVESWEPT: A trio of love stories by three of your favorite LOVESWEPT authors—Fayrene Preston, Kay Hooper, and Iris Johansen. **THE SHAMROCK TRINITY!** Fayrene, Kay, and Iris together "founded" the Delaney dynasty—its historical roots, principal members, settings, and present day heirs. (Those heirs are three of the most exciting men you'd ever want to meet in the pages of romances—Burke, York, and Rafe.) Armed with genealogies, sketches of settings, research notes they'd made on a joint trip to Arizona in which the books were to be set, each author then went off alone to create her own book in her own special style. There are common secondary characters, running gags through the three books. They can be read in any order, stand alone if the other two books are not read. Each book features appearances by the heroes of the other two books, each is set during the same span of time—and yet, no one gives away the end of the other books. This is a fascinating trinity of stories, indeed, very clever and well-crafted, and packing all the wallop you expect in a love story by Fayrene or Kay or Iris.

Don't miss these extraordinary love stories. Ask your bookseller to be sure to save the three books of **THE SHAMROCK TRINITY** for you. They are:

RAFE, THE MAVERICK
LOVESWEPT #167
By Kay Hooper

(continued)

YORK, THE RENEGADE
LOVESWEPT #168
By Iris Johansen

BURKE, THE KINGPIN
LOVESWEPT #169
By Fayrene Preston

Now, as I said above, there is an embarrassment of goodies around here. And four excellent examples are your LOVESWEPT romances for next month.

Leading off is witty Billie Green with **GLORY BOUND,** LOVESWEPT #155. Gloria Wainwright had a secret . . . and Alan Spencer, a blind date arranged by her matchmaking father, was a certain threat to keeping that secret. He was just too darned attractive, too irresistible, and the only way to maintain her "other life" was for Glory to avoid him—in fact, to disappear from Alan's world. But he tracked down the elusive lady whose various disguises hadn't repelled him as Glory intended, but only further intrigued him. When Alan and Glory come face to face in her bedroom—under the wildest circumstances imaginable—firecrackers truly do go off between these two. This romance is another sheer delight from Billie Green.

After a long absence from our list, the versatile Marie Michael is back with **NO WAY TO TREAT A LOVER,** LOVESWEPT #156. This is the fastpaced, exciting—often poignant—love story of beautiful Charley (short for Charlotte) Tremayne and the deliciously compelling Reese McDaniel. After a madly passionate affair, Charley had disappeared to follow a dangerous life of intrigue. Now, she and Reese are thrown together again on the stage of a musical bound for Broadway. Charley tries to stay away from Reese—for his safety!—but cannot resist him! You'll want to give both of these endearing people a standing ovation as they overcome Charley's fears . . . and a few other stumbling blocks fate throws in their way.

Peggy Webb's **DUPLICITY,** LOVESWEPT #157, is a delightfully humorous book that also will tug at your heartstrings. Dr. Ellen Stanford knows it is reckless to bring a perfect stranger home to pose as her fiance, but she just can't face another family reunion alone. Besides, the myste-

(continued)

rious Dirk is about as perfect as a man can get—as good looking as Tom Selleck, masterful yet tender, and one fabulous kisser! But Ellen is dedicated to her work, teaching sign language to a gorilla named Gigi, and Dirk is pledged to a way of life filled with dangerous secrets. How Dirk and Ellen work through their various deceptions will delight you and no doubt make you laugh out loud—especially when Gigi gets in the act as matchmaker!

Rounding out the month is another fabulous romance from Barbara Boswell! **ALWAYS AMBER,** LOVESWEPT #158, is a sequel to **SENSUOUS PERCEPTION,** LOVESWEPT #78. Remember Ashlee and Amber? They were the twins who were adopted in infancy by different families. In **SENSUOUS PERCEPTION,** Ashlee located her sister—and fell in love with Amber's brother. Now it's Amber's turn for romance. She has finally broken out of her shell and left the family banking business. The last person she expects to meet, much less be wildly attracted to, is Jared Stone, president of a bank that is her family's biggest rival. Amber doesn't quite trust Jared's intentions toward her, but can't deny her overwhelming need for him. You'll cheer Jared on as he passionately, relentlessly pursues Amber, until he finally breaks through her last inhibitions. . . . A breathless, delicious love story!

At long—wonderful—last the much awaited **SUNSHINE AND SHADOW** by Sharon and Tom Curtis will be published. This fabulous novel will be on sale during the first week of September. Be sure to look for it.

Have a glorious month of reading pleasure!

Warm regards,

Sincerely,

Carolyn Nichols

Carolyn Nichols
　Editor
LOVESWEPT
Bantam Books, Inc.
666 Fifth Avenue
New York, NY 10103

LOVESWEPT

*Love Stories you'll never forget
by authors you'll always remember*

LOVESWEPT

Love Stories you'll never forget by authors you'll always remember

- ☐ 21760 **Donovan's Angel #143** Peggy Webb $2.50
- ☐ 21761 **Wild Blue Yonder #144** Millie Grey $2.50
- ☐ 21762 **All Is Fair . . . #145** Linda Cajio $2.50
- ☐ 21763 **Journey's End #146** Joan Elliott Pickart $2.50
- ☐ 21751 **Once In Love With Amy #147** Nancy Holder $2.50
- ☐ 21749 **Always #148** Iris Johansen $2.50
- ☐ 21765 **Time After Time #149** Kay Hooper $2.50
- ☐ 21767 **Hot Tamales #150** Sara Orwig $2.50

Prices and availability subject to change without notice.

Buy them at your local bookstore or use this handy coupon for ordering:

Bantam Books, Inc., Dept. SW3, 414 East Golf Road, Des Plaines, Ill. 60016

Please send me the books I have checked above. I am enclosing $_____ (please add $1.50 to cover postage and handling). Send check or money order —no cash or C.O.D.'s please.

Mr/Mrs/Miss _____

Address _____

City _____ State/Zip _____

SW3—7/86

Please allow four to six weeks for delivery. This offer expires 1/87.